Anthology #2   Large Print
Hitchcock, Alfred
GRAVE SUSPICIONS

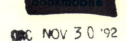

ALFRED HITCHCOCK'S
GRAVE SUSPICIONS
(Anthology II)

Edited by Cathleen Jordan

In these fifteen stories, only one thing
is certain; GRAVE SUSPICIONS II is
by far the most appropriate title for
this anthology. Anyone might have
designs on the life or loot of someone
else, and it is no easy matter to unmask
and then out-wit ... the thieves and
murderers that crowd these pages.

The tales collected here, in short –
all from the files of Alfred Hitchcock's
Mystery Magazine are ones that
whether you can unravel the crimes or
not, we hope you will enjoy.

ALFRED HITCHCOCK'S

Grave

Suspicion

Anthology II

Edited by Cathleen Jordan

John Curley & Associates, Inc.
South Yarmouth, Ma.

Library of Congress Cataloging-in-Publication Data
(Revised for volume 2)

Alfred Hitchcock's grave suspicions.
   Stories first published in Alfred Hitchcock's mystery
magazine.
   1. Detective and mystery stories, American.   2. Large
type books.   I. Jordan, Cathleen.   II. Grave suspicions.
[PS648.D4A343   1987]   813'0872'8   86–29176
ISBN 1–55504–281–3 (lg. print)
ISBN 1–55504–409–3 (soft: lg. print)

Published in Large Print by arrangement with Davis
Publications, Inc. in the United States and the rest of the
world market.

Distributed in the U.K. and Commonwealth by Magna
Print Books.

Printed in Great Britain

CONTENTS

ALFRED HITCHCOCK'S GRAVE SUSPICIONS
(Anthology II)

A Voice from the Leaves

by Donald Olson

Looking back over these past few weeks I realize that I never intended this to be a permanent arrangement – Cobb living with me here in Chicago, I mean. Call it selfish, but I fully expected him to go back to Fairhill when the new school term began, assuming of course that Sam McAllister had not in the meantime been arrested for murder. Now, whenever I drop hints to this effect, Cobb blandly ignores them with that inwardly meditative smile of his, the smile that makes him look like a teenage Talleyrand or like his great hero, Lawrence of Arabia, palavering with sly Bedouins under an eastern moon.

For a lad of fourteen Cobb has remarkable aplomb and presence, and when I see him stalking about this big apartment with *The Seven Pillars of Wisdom* under his arm and a look of sober deliberation on his face, I get the creepiest feeling that he's making plans to take over this place – as if it were some

1

strategic border area still in enemy hands; one of my more childish fantasies, since it implies that *I* am the enemy, which is absurd.

I first met Cobb McAllister when I returned to Fairhill for the first time in fourteen years in response to Sam's letter telling me that Cobb's mother was dead. Dead and buried, actually, and I thought it exactly like Sam to have been punctilious and feeling enough to inform me of Vinnie's death – but not in time for me to attend her funeral. Like most people who come from small rural towns, I'd cherished the illusion that nothing would have changed while I was away; the people, the quiet pace of life, the house where I was born, and especially that wilderness of heart-carved trees called Cobb's Woods, the enchanted playground of our youth. Yes, I clung to this last illusion despite common sense and Vinnie's last letter in which she'd reported that a midwestern firm had bought most of the acreage along the state road and planned to build a number of condominiums to be called Fairhill Farms.

As it was, trains no longer stopped at Fairhill and Sam had to drive all the way to Breezeford to meet me at the airport. Physically, he hadn't changed all that much, still wary-eyed and thin as whipcord, his manner as cool and self contained as when he and Vinnie Cobb and I had been such close chums. He'd never been much of a talker and the inhibiting sadness of the present reunion did not help break the ice as we drove to the village.

I did ask him if Vinnie had been ill for long before she died, but all he said was, "No, nothing like that," and I got the distinct feeling, despite his reticence, that he had a great deal on his mind and sooner or later would seek to unburden it.

We passed the Kidwell place and the livery stables, and as I had mentally prepared myself for the devastation of those holy places of my youth, not far up the road I was surprised and delighted when we approached Cobb's Woods and all that came into view was a single broken-window shell of a new apartment building, all brick and half-timbering, rising out of the long grass which all but hid a winding access road. Behind and around this solitary eyesore Cobb's Woods lay undisturbed in the sunset, evoking a flush of enchantment still strong enough to bring tears to my eyes – tears for Vinnie, for myself, for the lost sweet wonders of childhood brought back so vividly.

"They were going to put up a whole string of 'em," Sam explained, without my asking.

"What happened?"

3

"Company pulled out. Bad luck and bankruptcy."

We slowed down, waited for a truck to pass us, then swung across the road and into the drive of the old Cobb homestead where Sam and Vinnie had lived ever since their marriage.

"Cobb!" Sam's voice rang with urgency as he walked into the front parlor. "Where the devil's that kid got to?"

He went from room to room calling the boy, but no one answered.

"Relax," I said. "He'll show up."

"Kid's been told. Since all the trouble he knows he ain't supposed to wander off this time of day."

"Trouble?"

"Shootings. Killings. Vinnie didn't tell you?"

So he knew that Vinnie wrote to me. But that would have been like her, not to have deceived him about it.

"I haven't heard from Vinnie in months."

While another man might have reacted to this with dripping satire, Sam merely smiled his politely disbelieving and enigmatic smile.

"I mean it, Sam. I haven't."

He ignored the protest and told me about the "trouble." "All began with that infernal apartment project. Rumor said it was Mafia

4

money. But they say that about everything nowadays, even in these parts. Anyway, they built one, the one you saw. Then one of the bricklayers was shot dead. Figured it was a hunter's stray bullet, but then another one got it. And there was a rash of vandalism, one kind or another. Finally got it up, though. Couple of tenants moved in. One of 'em was shot dead, right through her bedroom window. Other was wounded. Paralyzed. Couldn't trace who did it. Figured they were shot with a rifle stolen from the Kidwell place when they were in Florida. High-powered job with a fancy Bushnell scope. Johnny Kidwell let me use it once when we went hunting together. Well, that put the lid on the project. Really spooked the deal. Nobody'd touch the place. Then the firm got into money troubles and that was the end. Everybody steers clear of there now. Even the kids. Except Cobb, of course. You can't keep him out of those woods. You remember how we were. He ain't no different."

Sam stood at the window looking across the state road at the fringe of trees in front of which you could just make out the faint golden wash of the setting sun on the brook where it straggled out of the glade and lost itself in the pastures of the outlying farms.

"It's that damned tree house," he

muttered. "I swear I've thought more than once of chopping it down out of there."

"*Our* tree house? It's still there?"

He gave me a rueful glance. "We built it to last forever, remember?"

The tree house. The heart of it all, the center of our activities, the symbol of all my happiest memories where golden summers cast their endless spells. I thought of it and I thought of Vinnie as she had looked at seventeen, clad only in green shadows up there among the leaves, smiling as she kissed me . . . that last perfect summer.

"You think Cobb's there now?"

Sam frowned. "I'll skin him alive if he is."

"I'll go look."

He protested, said I must be tired and would want to unpack and shower, but these were only excuses, I knew, and what really bothered him was that he wanted to talk about it, whatever it was, and here I was already rushing out of the house before I'd really got there; but I couldn't help it. More than anything else at that moment I wanted to see the tree house, the way it would look up there in the setting sun, which was so often the way it appeared in my Chicago reveries.

I crossed the road and the pasture into the shadows of the deep glade, following the brook to the big rock where forget-me-nots and shiny yellow cowslips grew as thickly as when I had waded upstream as a boy. I didn't try to scale the bank as I would have then, but followed the brook to the glade's end, then circled back toward the tree from behind.

I stopped under the branches and looked up. "Cobb? Cobb McAllister? You up there?"

Silence. Even the birds grew still, while all around me the smell of the woods and the textured pattern of the sunlight on the leaves were like keys that opened long-shut doors of memory.

I told him my name, whether or not it would mean anything to him, and said I'd helped build the tree house, and then I added: "Let me come up and I won't tell your dad you were here."

A voice came down to me out of the leaves: "Watch out below."

A thick knotted rope dropped at my feet. It appeared to be the same old rope. I gripped it and managed to scale the trunk to the lower branches, then clambered through them to the green-painted trapdoor, hauling myself through it to sprawl panting on the platform outside the one sizable room crammed with sleeping gear, candle stubs, ropes, knives, books, binoculars, tin plates and cups, all the essentials of tree house-keeping which hadn't changed since I'd spent so many happy hours there.

Vinnie had sent me pictures of Cobb at various stages of his development so I was not surprised to find him such a sturdy, handsome youth, big for his age and with an even more adult gravity of manner. He gave my hand a brief, unembarrassed shake. I offered my condolences. We chatted easily enough and presently I asked him if his mother had ever talked about me. He said, "Oh, sure. About all of you. All the fun you had. Heck, yes."

Surprising how many things hadn't changed. It might almost have been a shrine furnished with sacred relics. I reached out to the shelf for the Pyle *Robin Hood,* showing Cobb my name scribbled on the flyleaf. He smiled politely and I wondered if my excitement must strike him as silly in a grown man, for there was something about the watchful remoteness of his attitude that disconcerted me. I tried to act my age as I studied the view from the one small window facing west, straight across the treetops to the windows of the abandoned condominium.

"When I was last up here you could see all the way to the Overhead Bridge."

8

"Yeah, I know. Till they built that stupid apartment building. But we lucked out. They *were* going to build a whole mess of 'em."

Though the horizon was streaked with red, the glade below us was already thick with night shadows. "Your dad told me about the shootings. Aren't you scared being out here alone this time of day?"

He was quietly amused. "Why? Who'd want to kill me? Sometimes Vinnie and I'd stay here till after midnight, watching the stars."

Vinnie. I didn't like that. Children calling their parents by their Christian names is a modernism that always offends me.

On our way back to the house I asked him the same question I'd asked Sam: if Vinnie had been sick before she died.

Cobb's tone was tart, as if something smarted on his tongue. "He say she was sick?"

"Who?"

"Sam. Did he tell you that?"

"Not exactly."

"She wasn't ever sick. She fell. From the upstairs porch."

His words, or the quiet, offhand way he spoke them, chilled me as we passed out of the woods and along the brook flowing dark

9

as mercury through the gray-lit stubbly pasture.

"I hadn't heard from her for months."

His voice quickened. "She wrote to you?"

"Occasionally."

"What about?"

"Her painting. Things like that. You."

"What'd she say about me?"

"How proud she was of you. Mother stuff. You know."

"She sure did love the tree house," he said with a faraway, gentle conviction. "We used to spend an awful lot of time there." He kicked a branch out of the path. "*He* didn't like it." This last he said with an obscure but trenchant emphasis, and though I knew he was talking about Sam, I couldn't tell if he meant that Sam didn't like the tree house or didn't like their spending so much time there. Not for the first time in my life I felt a profound pity for Sam; it seemed his destiny always to be a third wheel.

"You don't blame him, do you, Cobb?" I felt impelled to ask him.

"For what?"

"For feeling that way about the tree house."

"Heck, no. I guess he's got a right."

We came to the barbed-wire fence along the road; he climbed over, I crawled under.

10

Before crossing the road he turned to look at me. "Tell me something, will you? Did he say she killed herself?"

"Good heavens, no."

"Because she didn't. My father killed her."

I couldn't have been more shocked, he said it with such utter authority. "You can't be serious, Cobb."

"No one could prove it, even if they tried. But just the same, he did. And he's going to pay for it. I'll see to that."

He opened the door for me. As I passed by him into the house, he added in a low voice, "Just thought you ought to know. In case something happens."

After supper Cobb disappeared to his room and Sam and I sat in the kitchen drinking beer and talking about the past, only now I wasn't so sure I wanted to hear whatever it was he was having such a hard time getting off his shoulders. I didn't believe what Cobb had said, but neither could I forget the shock of those words.

The clock struck midnight. I'd lost count of the number of beers Sam had drunk. At one point I asked him if I could look at Vinnie's old albums, all those snapshots of us as kids. He said he hadn't laid eyes on them for years, not since Cobb was a baby, that Vinnie must have stuck them away someplace. I said it didn't matter, but he insisted on looking for them and when he finally brought them to me he suggested I keep them. "I never look at them any more," he said.

As I turned the pages I began to notice something very odd: there wasn't a single picture in which I appeared; they had all been removed. I looked up at Sam but he wasn't paying any attention; in fact, his eyes were shut, and I was afraid he might fall asleep before imbibing enough courage to speak his mind.

"So Vinnie wasn't sick," I said rather sharply, and his eyes came open.

"No."

"Then how . . . ?"

"Killed herself."

I seemed to go on rocking involuntarily, as if the steady rhythm would soothe my pounding heart. "You can't mean that."

"Hell, I don't *know*. Not for sure."

He told me the story without my urging, how he'd gone looking for Vinnie one day just before dusk. She had gone for a walk and when it began to thunder and she hadn't come back he started to worry and walked up and down the state road looking for her. Then he'd taken it into his head that she

12

might have gone to the tree house. She had a thing about that tree house, he said, with just a trace of bitterness. Both her and the kid.

"It was just about dark when I got there. I called but she didn't answer. There was no reason to think she was up there, but I was sure she was. Don't ask me why. You live with someone fourteen years you get like that, reading each other's minds, sensing things. I kept calling. Then it hit me. I got to thinking maybe she was up there, but not alone. With somebody you know what I mean? I said, 'I'm coming up there, Vinnie.' That's when she spoke out. 'No!' she said, real scared like. 'Don't come up here! I'm coming down.' And the *way* she said it, you know . . . I never kidded myself about Vinnie. She was honest about it. Never once in them fourteen years did she say she loved me. She was always honest. That's what made it work for us. Honesty, I mean. It can be stronger than love. It holds up, you know. And when I heard her voice, scared like that, telling me not to come up there, I got this awful sick feeling that maybe she *hadn't* been all that honest. And lately, last few weeks, she'd been acting sort of funny, like she had something on her mind. Maybe all those years . . .

"I lost my fool head. I never get mad, not very often. You know that. But, hell, I'd

13

been so damned *good* to Vinnie. So damned fair. I'd done things for her no man in his right mind would have done. I said, 'I'm coming up there, Vinnie,' and I grabbed the rope and started pulling myself up when all of a sudden she fell. Or jumped. Without a word, without a cry. She was dead, that quick. And I still had to *know*, don't you see? I couldn't go through the rest of my life not ever being sure. So I left her there, wasn't nothing I could do for her, and I climbed to the tree house. . . . There was no one there."

He tilted his glass and emptied it in one long draft. "Well, I carried her home and made it look like she'd fallen from the porch up there. Don't ask me why. It just seemed more . . . fitting."

"Did anyone see you?"

"You mean Cobb? No. He was asleep in his room at the time."

"You sure?"

"Of course. Why? Did he say something?"

I couldn't bring myself to say it. "It's just his attitude."

"I know what you mean. He doesn't take to me. More like his mother. Books and stuff. That damned tree house. Ivory tower, that's what it was. For both of them. Cobb, he don't know one end of a fishing rod from the other. And he'd never go hunting with me

14

unless I practically forced him." His head sank lower, chin almost on his chest. He was quite drunk. "I'll never stop wondering. I'll always hear her voice coming down out of the leaves like that. Like rain, like birds in pain, or panic." After what seemed like a very long time he looked up at me, eye to eye. "I loved Vinnie. You know that. I couldn't show it, not with words. But I always loved her. I did what I could to prove it. She knew that."

I was touched, impressed, but more than anything else, confused. I felt so positive that he was leaving something out, or lacked the courage to tell me why it was so important to him that *I* should hear all this – and I would never find out, not that night. He was so drunk by then I had to put him to bed without knowing the full story.

The following day, a Saturday, I went up to the cemetery on Pine Ridge Road and laid some fresh forget-me-nots among the withering funeral bouquets on Vinnie's grave. Below me the village drowsed, the traffic hummed no louder than bees along the state road, the green mystery of Cobb's Woods looked in the near distance like one of Vinnie's delicate, sun-washed pastels. Heading in that direction, I skirted the condominium and seeing no one about I found an unlocked door and went inside. It was the usual sleazily built structure, small rooms, fake marble baths, miniature kitchens in shades of cocoa brown and avocado. From one of the top rooms I looked out across the long grass and undergrowth to Cobb's Woods, but it was impossible to pinpoint the tree house.

I found Cobb there, of course, at the tree house, his nose in a book. I offered him a candy bar, conscious as I did so that it was with almost the identical feeling I had placed those forget-me-nots on Vinnie's grave. As if it were a bribe, an apology, a plea for understanding if not forgiveness, and Cobb accepted the offering as if he knew this – which of course he could not.

We talked, among other things, about the aborted building project, Cobb explaining that the entire area had been scheduled for leveling and speaking proudly but not boastfully of his role in fighting the plan. "I helped circulate the petition against rezoning. Vinnie composed it. It was a real beaut. Lawyer couldn't have done a better job. It *was* against the law, you know, building that apartment house. The neighborhood had to be rezoned first. We got over a hundred names against it. But they had the money. They bought off the mayor and his cronies. Vinnie was really broken up about it. This tree house meant everything to her. She always said everyone ought to have a secret place where they could store their dreams and memories and know they'd always be there when they wanted them."

Such talk made me uneasy. I said, "Do you think they'll ever catch whoever did the shootings?"

"I sure hope not."

He laughed at my surprise. "Well, heck, look at it this way. Whoever pulled the trigger, it was the mayor and his pals who were responsible. They didn't have any right rezoning this area."

Sam's words came back to me: *I'd done things for her no man in his right mind would have done. . . . I always loved her. I did what I could to prove it.* I tried to believe that I was giving those words an arbitrary meaning.

"Was your mother pleased?"

Cobb's expression faltered, as if the candy bar he was munching had turned bitter in his mouth. "It saved the tree house, didn't it?"

"I asked you if she was pleased?"

"Look!" he suddenly cried. "There's McNutt, my pet squirrel. I'll bet he smelled my candy bar."

That afternoon, knowing I had to get back to Chicago by the following day, I was

17

determined to bring things to a head, and when Sam and I were alone, I mentioned what Cobb had said about the rezoning business. "I guess Vinnie did all she could to preserve that tree house."

His lower lip jerked forward. "Vinnie was a dreamer. I could have told her it wouldn't do no good."

"But violence did."

His eyes were wide open but giving nothing away. "Sometimes that's what it takes."

"Yet it was all for nothing. She didn't live to enjoy it." I was prompting him as boldly as I dared, but perhaps he'd changed his mind; perhaps he'd decided he couldn't trust me after all. This possibility made me angry enough to prod him even more bluntly.

"Listen, Sam. Don't think I'm not aware of what I owe you. I've never forgotten. I'm willing to repay you any way I can. If you need help all you have to do is ask. If you've done something and it's bothering you and you want to talk about it, I'm ready to listen. And I give you my word. It'll go no further."

He looked at me rather strangely as I said this, and then, dropping his gaze, he loudly cleared his throat.

"You got somebody with you? In Chicago?"

"You mean living with me?" I grinned. "Not at the moment, as it happens."

"Take him with you."

It caught me unprepared, maybe because I was expecting, if anything, a more explicit confession.

"Please," he said. "Just for a while, anyway. At least till school starts."

"Why, Sam?"

"Better for him. All this moping and brooding ain't good for him. He needs a change."

The reticence of the man went too deep; he wasn't the confessing sort, and I had no right to badger him.

Nevertheless, I said, "He thinks you killed Vinnie."

"That's a lie."

"I know that. Maybe you'd have done anything *for* her.... I know you wouldn't have done anything *to* her."

His voice was blade sharp. "That's not what I meant. I meant it's not true he thinks I killed Vinnie."

"It's what he told me."

"You're wrong. You must have misunderstood him." He backed away, and I realized that we'd been standing toe to toe, like boxers. "What the hell, it don't matter. Will you take him away? Or will you run true to form and do your damnedest to avoid responsibility?"

I deserved that. I let it pass. "Will he come?"

"Only one reason he wouldn't. That damned tree house."

Our eyes met, and I knew what I must do. It was true, of course. If Sam was in danger of being exposed, the boy would be better off out of it all, away from him.

It took me less time than I thought, even though I probably worked harder than necessary knowing that I had to get it done before Cobb finished his chores and headed for the tree house. My emotions while I was doing it were as confused as my motives. It seemed to me that when I would pause in my exertions it was Vinnie's voice I could hear in the leaves around me, crying out against what I was doing, and I would be struck by a terrible sense of loss and shame and betrayal, and would have to whisper to myself: "It's only the wind in the leaves; it's only the wind."

Later, at the house, I didn't hear Cobb when he came in because I was upstairs packing, and it wasn't until I heard their voices ripping into each other that I went to the door and listened, and when I went down

20

I found them squared off and furious in the middle of the kitchen.

"You're lying!" Cobb screamed. "I know you did it. You always said you'd tear it down. You hated it!"

If he'd been dead Sam's face couldn't have looked more like a corpse's.

Cobb turned to me in a frenzy. "He did! He destroyed the tree house! Vinnie's tree house. Our secret place. He said he would and now he's gone and done it. He was always jealous!"

"Not of you, boy," Sam murmured. "Never of you."

When there was nothing left between them but a bitter residue of hostility I took my cue and spoke quietly, reasonably, setting forth my proposition that maybe Cobb would like to come to Chicago with me for a while, an invitation to which he promptly agreed, without a moment's forethought, almost as if he had expected it, and Sam's eyes met mine in a secret smile of victory.

I had made up my mind to say nothing to Cobb about the past, with one exception, which my conscience insisted be made. On the plane I told him that I was sure he was mistaken about his father.

"What do you mean?" he said.

21

"He didn't kill your mother. You mustn't believe that."

"Oh, yes. He killed her."

"That's simply not true, Cobb."

His voice was as reasonable and patient as if he were explaining algebra to a poet. "I don't mean that *he* pushed her off the porch. But that doesn't mean he didn't kill her. Like those other people that were killed. The mayor and his buddies didn't actually shoot them, but it was still their fault. My father's an evil man. He never did the right thing by Vinnie or me. But he'll be sorry. He's going to pay for it. You wait and see."

Neither of us made any further reference to that conference and for a while I thought that bringing Cobb to Chicago had been an excellent idea, that all he had really needed was to get away from Fairhill and the tree house, and Sam. Naturally, I wondered if Cobb could suspect that Sam had shot all those people, but I've come to believe that he does not. Cobb has been with me nearly a month now, and when I mention Sam's name to see if his hostility toward him has diminished, he seems hardly to remember whom I'm talking about – or so he pretends, at least. I think that if he did suspect Sam he would have dropped some hint to that effect, even if he condoned and admired Sam for it. After all, he had been quick enough to accuse Sam of killing his mother.

Strike that last sentence. As it happens, I was wrong even about that. Two weeks have passed since I wrote those words and much has happened, so much that I'm almost too stunned to grasp its full significance. The evidence is there, I've seen it with my own eyes, so what else *can* I believe? Yet it's all so grotesque, so appalling, I find myself refusing to accept it, for though I believe in the *existence* of evil – it's all around us, I'm sure – this particular manifestation of it is simply too horrendous to conceive.

First, I'd better explain that on the surface nothing happened to disturb my peace of mind during the first week or so that Cobb was here. I'd let him do pretty much as he pleased and we seemed to take pleasure in each other's company. I'd told him to treat the apartment as his home, although I hadn't quite that degree of independence in mind that he gradually appropriated. I didn't mind his making a point of always locking his bedroom door whether he was in there or not – boys can often be funny about that sort of thing – but I did think he might have been more heedful of my warnings about wandering around Chicago after dark. After all, I told him, it isn't exactly Fairhill, and that he looks so much older than he is would, if anything, increase the risk he might be taking. All he said in reply was that he was looking for something, something he had to find as soon as possible, and yet he refused to tell me what it was, saying only that it would be a surprise.

As to the evidence I mentioned, this is how it came to light: Cobb had gone out for the afternoon, locking his bedroom door behind him as usual, and I was in my study working on a report when I discovered I needed to refer to some data packed away in the closet in Cobb's room. I'd never bothered to mention that I had a duplicate key to his door – I think he knew I would respect his privacy even if I had – and I unlocked the door and was rummaging about in the closet looking for the particular file I needed when I noticed a shirt on the floor in the corner. Thinking it must have fallen from a hanger I started to pick it up when I found that it was wrapped carefully around a small wooden box.

Not meaning to pry, but simply curious, I opened the box and found two things inside: a small package wrapped in brown paper, and an expensive Bushnell rifle scope. Call it memory, call it instinct, call it anything you want, I knew at once, and infallibly, that it was the scope stolen from the Kidwell place and used in the shootings at Fairhill Farms.

At the same time I knew that I was wrong about Sam, as if by holding that scope to my eye I could see what actually happened, could see Vinnie, tormented by suspicion, going to the tree house alone at dusk and finding the rifle and scope hidden there, and suddenly Sam was there, threatening to come up, and I could picture her terror and panic, her fear of having Sam discover what Cobb had done. In such blind distress she would have done anything to stop Sam – yes, I think she would even have jumped – but Sam had climbed to the tree house anyway, not looking for a gun, which he might not have noticed even if it was there, but for a man, a rival.

Yes, it all could have happened like that, or if not exactly like that, then in some way not so very different. There was, of course, another possibility, one which I refused even to let myself consider, for after all Cobb is only a boy, he's not a monster. He might have been capable of stealing a rifle and shooting strangers in one mad last resort to preserve his beloved tree house, but if his mother had somehow discovered what he had done and reacted in a way that had angered or displeased him, he still would not have been capable of harming her himself. That idea is unthinkable.

Four more days have passed, giving me time to reflect on my discoveries, and more of the pattern has become clear, almost all of it, and I'm beginning to understand how totally I've deceived myself. Sam knows the truth, of that I'm almost certain; nothing else would explain his behavior, or the things he said which I was so quick to misconstrue. His single purpose in calling me to Fairhill must have been to persuade me to take Cobb away from there, not only because that whole bad scene only nourished the boy's paranoia, or whatever one wished to call it, but because sooner or later he might be driven to some other act that would ultimately expose him to the authorities. Why Sam had not been more frank with me I can't be sure. Perhaps he doesn't trust me; after all, he never did.

Something else now: that other item in the box. When I unwrapped that small package I found what in some ways was an even greater shock to me than the gun scope – a collection of all those snapshots from Vinnie's album, the ones in which I was pictured. Now, Sam would never have told

26

Cobb the truth about me, at least I don't think he would have, and I'm even more sure that the boy would never have learned anything from Vinnie; in fact, she must have hidden those albums away to be sure he would never come across those pictures and guess the truth. Obviously, he *had* found them. Then what? Had he faced Vinnie with them, one day up there in the tree house? Vinnie would not have lied, I'm sure of that. Later on, needing someone on whom to place the burden of guilt for his mother's death, regardless how it had happened, what could be more logical than to have chosen his father, just as he had blamed the other deaths on the "mayor and his buddies."

For you see, Cobb never did accuse *Sam* of killing his mother. What he'd said, with such curious emphasis and precision, with such diabolical candor and subtle duplicity was that his *father* had killed Vinnie; and on the plane he'd been so careful to say, "My *father's* an evil man. He never did right by Vinnie and me. But he'll be sorry. He's going to pay for it. You wait and see."

You wait and see. Even then I should have seen through his grim little joke.

I should have realized what he was telling me when he referred to his *father* both those times, for he never called Sam his father, any

27

more than he called Vinnie by anything but her Christian name. He was talking about the person in those snapshots, the person who looked so startlingly like himself.

He was talking about his real father. About me.

Cobb came in a few minutes ago, stuck his head in the study door and waved a small package, announcing very gaily that he'd found what he was looking for – finally.

"What is it?" I asked.

He only laughed. "I told you. A surprise." Then, as if it were the biggest joke in the world, he added: "Actually, it's for my father. He'll really get a charge out of it."

With that he disappeared into his room, locking the door behind him, of course, and I've been sitting here trying to make myself believe that my reasoning about all this is absurd, way off the track, preposterous, and for all I know maybe it is. I certainly don't want to panic myself into the blunder of opening my mouth and saying a lot of things I'd later regret. There's no point in trying to excuse my past behavior if I don't have to, of trying to make him understand that it wasn't that I didn't *want* to marry Vinnie when she became pregnant with my child. I simply wasn't ready for all that. I had

28

dreams, plans, ambitions. Vinnie under-
stood. She never blamed me. She never
stopped loving me, either, which is probably
why they hate me.

If they do hate me, both Sam and Cobb,
is it remotely, wildly conceivable that they've
been acting together in all this? That they
have, for their own madly inscrutable
reasons, *set me up?*

No, I must be mistaken. How could there
possibly have been a gun in that package he
waved in front of me? Just because he may
have succeeded in stealing a rifle and scope
in Fairhill doesn't mean he would have the
skill to swipe a handgun in Chicago. He's
clever, yes, but hardly that clever.

I've given up on the report; I can't
possibly concentrate with that rock music
blasting through the wall of Cobb's room.
I can't imagine what's got into the kid, he
never had it that loud before. He's always
been the soul of courtesy and thoughtful-
ness.

I really must do something about it, but
for some reason I have the strongest
reluctance to get up and walk to his door and
tell him to please turn it down. Not that it
would do any good; he'd never hear me. Not
even a cannon could be heard over that
frightful din.

29

Now his door is opening, very, very slowly. And would you believe it? He's turned that volume up even *higher!*

This Day's Evil

by Jonathan Craig

It had been a near thing. It had been so near that even now, as he crouched there in the bushes behind the small frame house of the man he had come to kill, there was still a taut queasiness in his stomach, and the sweat that laved his ribs was chill.

Half an hour ago, he had been five minutes away from murder. He had stood at the back door of the house, one hand on the heavy automatic in his pocket, the other raised to knock. Then, through the barred but open window, he had heard the hollow pound of heavy boots across the front porch, the hammering of a big man's fist on the door, and the lazy rise and fall of Sheriff Fred Stratton's sing-song voice calling out a greeting to the man inside.

"Charlie!" Stratton had said in that fond, bantering tone he always used with Charlie Tate, "Charlie, you no-good rascal, your time has come. Open the door before I break it down."

31

He hadn't heard Charlie's reply. He had already been running toward the bushes in the back yard, his knees rubbery and his stomach knotting spasmodically with the realization that if the sheriff had come five minutes later he would have caught him in the house with a dead man.

Now, hidden from the house by the bushes, his fear-sharpened senses acutely aware of the incessant drone of insects and the sickening sweetness of lilacs, Earl Munger shifted his weight very slowly and carefully, trying to still the tremor in his legs.

To have been caught in the act by that lazy, fat slob of a sheriff would have been just his luck, he reflected. Sheriff Fred Stratton was the laziest, slowest man in the county, with a maddening, syrupy drawl that made you want to jam your hand down his throat and pull the words out for him.

They made a good pair, Fred Stratton and Charlie Tate. Stratton had lots of fat, and Tate had lots of money. Not that Tate would have the money long; just as soon as the sheriff left, Tate would have neither the money nor his life.

There were sure some strange ducks in this world, Earl thought sourly. Take Charlie, now. Here he was, seventy if he was a day, with nobody knew how much money hidden in his house, and living like a pauper. He didn't trust anybody or anything, unless maybe it was the sheriff, and he especially didn't trust banks. If all the cash money he'd collected in rent from the property he owned all over the county was in the house, as it almost had to be, there'd be something pretty close to fifty thousand dollars. Charlie never spent a dime. He was a crazy old miser, with bars and bolts on every door and window, just like in the story books, and for all the good his money did him, he might just as well be dead.

And he would be, Earl promised himself again. The money might not do any good for Charlie, but it would sure do a lot of good for him. At twenty-three, he owned the clothes he had on, and another outfit just like them, and nothing more. But after today things would be different. There'd be no more conversations like that one night before last with Lois Kimble, when he'd asked her to go for a drive with him.

"A drive?" Lois had said, the perfect doll's face as innocent as a child's. "A drive in *what*, Earl?"

"The truck," he had said. "It's more comfortable than it looks."

"You mean that old thing you haul fertilizer around in all day?"

"It doesn't smell," he said. "If it did, I wouldn't ask you."

"I'll bet."

"It doesn't. And it rides real good, Lois. You'd be surprised."

She looked at him for a long moment, the wide grey eyes inscrutable. "I'd be ashamed," she said. "I really would, Earl."

"You figure you're too good to ride in a truck? Is that it?"

She started to turn away. "I meant I'd be ashamed if I were you," she said. "I'd be ashamed to ask a girl to... Oh, it doesn't matter anyhow. I've got to be going, Earl."

"Sure, it matters. Listen –"

"Not to me," she said, walking away from him. "Goodbye, Earl."

And an hour later he had seen her pass the feed store where he worked, beautiful in her thin summer dress, wide grey eyes fixed attentively on the well-dressed young man beside her, the low-slung red sports car growling arrogantly through the town as if it were affronted by the big unwashed sedans at the curbs, impatient to be back with its own kind in the city where the bright lights and the life and the pleasure were, where there were places that charged more for a dinner than Earl made in a week.

But after today, all that would be changed.

34

He'd have to wait a cautious time, of course, and then he could leave the stink of the feed store and the town far behind, and the young man in the sharp clothes and the red sports car with the beautiful girl on the seat beside him would be none other than Earl Munger.

This afternoon, he had rushed his deliveries so that he would have a full hour to kill and rob Charlie Tate before his boss at the feed store would begin to wonder where he was. He had hidden the small panel truck in the woods back of Charlie's place and then approached the house by a zigzag course through brush and trees, certain that no one had seen him, and that he could return to the truck the same way.

He wondered now why he hadn't robbed Charlie before, why he'd waited so long. And yet, with another part of his mind, he knew why. To rob Charlie, it would be necessary to kill him. The only way to get into his house was to have Charlie unlock the door, and Charlie couldn't be left alive to tell what had happened.

Then he heard the muffled slam of Charlie's front door, and a few moments later the sudden cough and roar of a car engine on the street out in front, and he knew that Sheriff Stratton had left.

Now! Earl thought as he left the bushes

and moved swiftly to the back door. I can still do it and be back at the store before anybody starts getting his suspicions up. Once again he closed one hand over the automatic in his pocket and raised the other to knock.

Charlie Tate's footsteps shuffled slowly across the floor, and a moment later his seamed, rheumy-eyed face peered out at Earl through the barred opening in the upper half of the door.

"Hello, Earl," he said. "What is it?"

"The boss asked me to bring you something, Mr. Tate," Earl said, glancing down as if at something beyond Charlie's angle of vision.

"That so?" Charlie said. "What?"

"I don't know," Earl said. "It's wrapped up."

"I didn't order anything," Charlie said.

"It's too big to stick through those bars, Mr. Tate," Earl said. "If you'll open the door, I'll just shove it inside."

Charlie's eyes studied Earl unblinkingly for a full ten seconds; then there was a grating sound from inside, and the door opened slowly, and not very far.

But it was far enough. Earl put his hip against it, forced it back another foot, and slipped inside, the gun out of his pocket now

36

and held up high enough for Charlie to see it at once.

There was surprise on Charlie's face, but no fear. "What do you think you're doing?" he asked.

"I'm taking your money," Earl said. "Wherever it is, get it, and get it now."

Charlie took a slow step backward. "Don't be a fool, son," he said.

"Don't you," Earl said. "It's your money or your life, Charlie. Which'll it be?"

"Son, I –"

Earl raised the gun a little higher. "Get it," he said softly. "You understand me, Charlie? I'm not asking you again."

Charlie hesitated for a moment, then turned and moved on uncertain feet to the dining room table. "It's in there," he said, his breathy, old-man's voice almost inaudible. There was a bottle of whisky on the table, but no glasses.

"In the table?" Earl said. "I'm telling you, Charlie. Don't try to pull –"

"Under the extra leaves," Charlie said. "But listen, son –"

"Shut up," Earl said, lifting one of the two extra leaves from the middle of the table. "I'll be damned."

There were two flat steel document cases
37

wedged into the shallow opening formed by the framework beneath the leaves.

Earl pulled the other leaf away and nodded to Charlie. "Open them," he said.

"You can still change your mind," Charlie said. "You can walk out of here right now, and I'll never say any –"

"Open them, I said!"

Charlie sighed heavily, fumbled two small keys from his pocket, and opened the document cases.

It was there, all right, all in neat, banded packages of twenties and fifties, each of the packages a little over two inches thick.

The size of his haul stunned him, and it was several seconds before he could take his eyes from it. Then he remembered what else had to be done and he looked questioningly at the wall just over Charlie Tate's left shoulder.

"What's that?" he asked. "What've you got *there*, Charlie?"

His face puzzled, Charlie turned to look. "What are you talking . . . ?" he began, and then broke off with an explosive gasp as the butt of Earl's automatic, with the full strength of Earl's muscular arm and shoulder behind it, crashed against his skull just two inches behind his right ear.

He fell to the floor without a sound, all of

a piece, the way a bag of old clothes held at arm's length would fall, in a limp heap.

Earl knelt down beside him, raising the gun again. Then he lowered it and shoved it back into his pocket. Nobody would ever have to hit Charlie Tate again.

He started to rise, then sank back, the sudden nervous tightening of the muscles across his stomach so painful that he winced. It was all he could do to drag himself to the table. He uncapped the bottle of whisky and raised it to his lips, shaking so badly that a little of the liquor sloshed out onto the table. It was a big drink, and it seemed to help almost at once. He took another one, just as big, and put the bottle back down on the table.

It was then that he heard the car door slam shut out front, and saw, above the sill of the front window, the dome light and roof-mounted antenna of Sheriff Fred Stratton's cruiser.

A moment before, Earl Munger would have sworn he could not move at all, but he would have been wrong. He moved too quickly to think, too quickly to feel. It took him less than five seconds to close the document cases and shove them under his arm, and it took him even less time than that to reach the back door and close it soundlessly behind him. Returning to the truck by the roundabout route that would prevent his being seen took the better part of ten minutes, every second of it a desperate fight against an almost overpowering urge simply to cut and run.

He'd left the truck on an incline, so that he would be able to get it under way again without using the starter. Now he pushed the shift lever into the slot for second gear, shoved in the clutch, released the hand brake, waited until the truck had rolled almost to the bottom of the incline, and then let the clutch out. The engine caught, stuttered, died, then caught again, and he drove away as slowly, and therefore as quietly, as he could without stalling the engine again.

Half a mile farther on, he turned off onto a rutted side road that led to a small but deep lake known locally as Hobbs Pond. There he shoved the gun and the packages of money into a half-empty feed sack, making sure they were well covered with feed, and then sent the metal document cases arching as far toward the center of the lake as he could throw them.

Then, after burying the bag under half a dozen other bags of feed and fertilizer in the truck, he started back toward the store. The money would probably be safe in the truck for as long as he wanted to leave it there, but there was no sense in taking any chances. Tonight or tomorrow he would bury it somewhere, and then leave it there until the day when he could pick a fight with his boss, quit his job, and leave the area for good without raising any questions.

Back at the store, Burt Hornbeck came out on the front loading platform and eyed him narrowly.

"Didn't I see you gassing up that truck at Gurney's this morning?" he asked.

"That's right," Earl said.

"Well, how come? You ever know Gurney to buy anything from this store?"

"No."

"You bet, 'no.' What Gurney buys, he buys at Ortman's. Next time, gas it up at Cooper's, like I told you. Coop buys here, and so I buy from Coop. Got it?"

"The tires needed air," Earl said. "Coop hasn't got any air hose."

"Never mind the air hose. After this, gas that truck up at Coop's. I'm beginning to wonder how many times I got to tell you."

Not too many times, Earl thought as he walked back to the washroom to throw cold water on his face. Another couple or three weeks, a month at the most, and he'd be

41

buying gas for a sassy red sports car, not a battered old delivery truck.

The whisky had begun to churn in his stomach a little. But it would be all right, he knew. From now on, everything would be all right. For a man with thousands of dollars everything had to be. That was the way of the world.

When he came back out to the loading platform, Sheriff Stratton's car was there, and the sheriff was talking with a fair-sized knot of men. The sheriff was sitting on the old kitchen chair Hornbeck kept out on the platform, his enormous bulk dwarfing it, making it seem like something from a child's playroom.

Trust the fat slob not to stand up when he can sit down, Earl thought as he edged a bit closer. The laziest man in the county, if not in the state. If Stratton was on one side of the street and wanted to get to the other, he would climb in his car, drive to the corner, make a U-turn, and come back, all to save walking a lousy forty feet. And talk about fat. The county could save money by buying a tub of lard and nailing a star on it. They'd have just as good a sheriff, and it wouldn't cost them a fraction of what they had to pay Stratton.

"What happened?" Earl asked George

Dill, who had wandered over from his grocery store.

"It's old Charlie Tate," George said. "He's done took poison."

"He *what?*" Earl said.

"Poison," George said. "He killed himself."

The sheriff glanced up at Earl and nodded. "Howdy, Earl," he said, making about six syllables out of it. "Yes, that's what he did, all right. Lord only knows why, but he did." Beneath his immaculate white Stetson, the sheriff's round, pink-skinned face was troubled, and the small, almost effeminate hands drummed nervously on his knees.

"He – poisoned himself?" Earl said.

"I always said he was crazy, and now I know it," Norm Hightower, who owned the creamery, said. "He'd have to be."

There were a dozen questions Earl wanted to ask, but he could ask none of them. He wet his lips and waited.

The sheriff took a small ivory-colored envelope from the breast pocket of his shirt, looked at it, shook his head wonderingly, and slipped it back into his pocket.

"Charlie gave me that about half an hour before I found him dead," he said. "He told me not to open it until after supper. But there was something about the way he said it that bothered me. He tried to make it sound like maybe he was playing a little joke on somebody, maybe me. But he didn't bring it off. I had this feeling, and so as soon as I got around the corner I stopped the car and read it."

"And it said he was going to kill himself?" Joe Kirk, who carried the Rural Route One, said.

"That's what it said, all right," the sheriff said.

"But he didn't say why?" Frank Dorn, the barber, asked.

"No," Stratton said. "All he said was, he was going to do it, and what with." He reached into his right-hand trouser pocket and drew out a small blue and yellow tin about the size of a package of cigarettes. "And that's another thing I can't understand, boys. It's bad enough he would want to kill himself. But why would he do it with a thing like this?"

"What is it?" Sam Collins, from the lumberyard, asked.

"Trioxide of arsenic," the sheriff said, putting the tin back in his pocket. "I found it on the floor beneath the table."

"How's that again, sheriff?" Sam Collins asked.

"Ratsbane, Sam," Stratton said. "Arsenic.

I reckon there isn't a more horrible death in this world than that. It must be the worst agony there is."

"Why'd he want to take such a thing, then?" Jim Ryerson, the mechanic from Meckle's Garage asked.

"It's like I told you," Norm Hightower said. "He was crazy. I always said so, and now I know it."

The sheriff got to his feet, ponderously, looking at the now badly-sprung kitchen chair regretfully, as if he hated to leave it. "Well," he drawled in that slow, slow singsong of his, "I reckon maybe I'd better call the coroner and the others. At least Charlie didn't have any kin. It seems like kinfolks just can't stand the idea of somebody killing himself. They always carry on something fierce. I've even had them try to get me to make out they died a natural death or got killed somehow. Anything but suicide. They can't stand it at all."

"I fed arsenic to some rats once," Tom Martin, the druggist, said. "I'd never do it again. When I saw what it did to those rats, I . . . well, I'd never do it again. Even rats don't deserve to die like that. It was the most awful thing I ever saw."

"Like I said before," the sheriff said. "I

just can't understand old Charlie killing himself that way."

"Maybe he didn't know exactly what it would do to him," Tom Martin said.

"Maybe not," the sheriff said. "I don't see how he could know, and still take half a box of ratsbane and dump it in a bottle of whisky and drain almost half of it. There must have been enough arsenic in that bottle to kill everybody here and half the other folks in town besides." He moved off slowly in the direction of his car, picking his way carefully, as if to complete the short trip in the fewest steps possible. "I'd better be seeing about those phone calls," he said. "There's always a big to-do with a thing like this. Of course, Charlie's not having any kin is a help, but there'll still be a lot of work."

On the loading platform, Earl Munger tried to fight back the mounting terror inside him. No wonder the sheriff had taken one look at Charlie Tate lying there on the floor and thought he had died of poison. Why should he have looked for wounds or anything else? And how long would it be, Earl wondered, before the ratsbane really did to him what the sheriff had thought it had done to Charlie Tate? It was already killing him, he knew; he would feel the first horrible clutch of agony at any moment.

46

He forced himself to walk with reasonable steadiness to the truck, and although the door felt as heavy as the door of a bank vault, he managed to open it somehow and get in and drive away slowly.

Once on the highway that led to Belleville, he mashed the gas pedal to the floorboard and kept it there. He had to get to a doctor, and in this forsaken area doctors were few and very far between. The nearest was Doc Whittaker, four miles this side of Belleville. Whittaker might be a drunk but he knew his business, at least when he was sober.

But when he reached Whittaker's place, Mrs. Whittaker told him her husband was out on a house call. He half ran back to the truck, already stabbing with the ignition key as he jumped inside, and took off with a scorch of rubber that left Mrs. Whittaker staring after him with amazement.

The next nearest doctor was Courtney Hampton, six miles east of Belleville on Coachman Road.

He was beginning to feel it now, the first stab of pain deep in the pit of his stomach. It wasn't like the other pains, the ones he had felt earlier when he was scared; it wasn't as acute, but it was growing stronger, and it was deep, deep inside him. It was the arsenic, and it was going to kill him.

There was a red light ahead. The Belleville cutoff. He kept the gas pedal on the floor, and when he reached the intersection, he shut his eyes for a moment, waiting for the collision that was almost sure to come. Brakes screamed and tires squealed on both sides of him, but no one crashed into him, and he started down the long, straight stretch of highway that would bring him to Coachman Road.

Eighteen minutes later, Earl Munger sat on Dr. Hampton's operating table, a rubber tube in his stomach, while the doctor filled a hypodermic needle, and then, without Earl's feeling it at all, inserted it in the back of his upper arm.

"And so you spread your lunch out right there where the insect spray could get to it," Hampton said, almost with amusement. "And sat there eating sandwiches garnished with arsenic, without even knowing it."

He glanced at Earl as if he expected him to say something, tube in his stomach or not. "Well," he went on, "you wouldn't be able to tell, of course. That's the insidious thing about arsenic. There's no smell or taste. That's why it's been a poisoner's favorite all through the ages."

"You want me to come back again, doc?"

Earl asked when Hampton had removed the tube.

"Not unless you feel ill again," Hampton said. "That will be ten dollars, please."

On his way home, Earl Munger, for the first time in his life, knew the meaning of pure elation. It was a strange feeling, one he couldn't quite trust at first; but with every mile the feeling grew, and the happiness that flooded through him was the kind of happiness he had known as a child when things and people were the way they seemed to be, and not, as he had learned all too soon, the way they really were.

He took the long curve above the old Haverman place almost flat out, feeding more gas the farther he went into it, the way he had read that sports car drivers did. Even the old delivery truck seemed to handle like a sports car, and it amused him to think that, with the way he and the truck felt just now, he could show those fancy Ferrari and Lotus and Porsche drivers a thing or two.

He felt like singing, and he did. He felt like a fool; he felt as if he were drunk, but he sang at the top of his voice, and he was still singing when he braked the truck to a stop in front of the feed store and got out.

He would take the long way home, he decided. It was the better part of two miles that way, but he felt like walking, something he hadn't felt like doing in more years than he could remember.

He began to sing again, walking slowly, enjoying himself to an extent he would once have believed impossible. He sang all the way to his rooming house, and then, just as happily but a bit more quietly, continued to sing as he climbed the stairs to his room on the second floor and opened the door.

Sheriff Fred Stratton sat there in Earl's only chair, the pink moonface as expressionless as so much suet, the small hands lying quietly on the brim of the spotless white Stetson in his lap.

Earl stared at him for a moment, then closed the door and sat down on the side of the bed. "What are you doing here, sheriff?" he asked.

"We were waiting for you at the store," Stratton said. "My deputy and me."

"I didn't see anybody," Earl said. "Why would you be wait –?"

"We didn't mean for you to see us," Stratton said. "It didn't take us long to find that money, Earl. And the gun too, of course."

"Money?" Earl said. "What money? I don't know anything about any money. Or any gun, either."

50

Stratton reached up and took the small, ivory-colored envelope from the breast pocket of his shirt. "Letter from my youngest daughter," he said. "Looks like she's bound and determined to make me a proud granddaddy again."

"That's the same letter you told everybody Charlie Tate gave you just before he –" Earl began, then broke off abruptly.

"That's right," Stratton said, putting the envelope back in his pocket and taking out the small blue and yellow tin. "Just like I told them this little box of throat lozenges was ratsbane."

Earl felt his mouth go dry. "Not poison?" he heard himself say. "Not arsenic?"

"No," Stratton said. "And even if Charlie *had* been meaning to poison himself, he wouldn't have put the poison in a bottle of whisky. He never took a drink in his life. That bottle on the table was mine, son. Charlie always kept a bottle on hand for me, because he knew I was a man that liked a little nip now and then."

Stratton glanced down at the tin.

"I dropped this at Charlie's house when I was there the first time, and so I went back to get it. When I saw what had happened, and that Charlie had opened his back door to somebody, I knew the killer had to be a

51

man he knew pretty well. Otherwise, Charlie would never have let him in the house."

"But why?" Earl asked. "Why did you...?"

"Why'd I make up all that about the letter and the lozenges?" Stratton said. "Well, I got the idea when I noticed the killer had helped himself to the whisky. I'd had a drink myself, the first time I was there, and I could see that somebody had taken it down another couple of inches, not to mention spilling some on the table. I figured the killing must have rawed somebody's nerves so much he'd had to take a couple of strong jolts to straighten himself out."

Stratton paused, studying Earl with tired, sleepy eyes that told him nothing at all. Earl waited until he could wait no longer. "And then?" he asked.

"Well," Stratton said, "there's one sure thing in this world, son. A man that thinks he's been poisoned is going to get himself to a doctor, and get there fast. And since there're only four doctors within thirty miles of here, all I had to do was call them and ask them to let me know who showed up."

"But I had the symptoms," Earl said. "I was in pain, and I –"

"Sometimes if a man *thinks* a thing is so, then it *is* so," Stratton said. "You were dead

52

certain you'd been poisoned, and so naturally you had the symptoms."

He got to his feet, put the big white hat on his head very carefully, and gestured toward the door. "Well, Earl, I reckon we'd better head over toward the jail."

"A trap," Earl said bitterly. "A dirty, lousy trap. I guess you figure you're pretty smart, don't you?"

Stratton looked surprised.

"No such thing," he said. "Just pretty lazy. I saw a chance to make your guilty conscience do my work for me, and I took it. That's how it is with us lazy folks, son. If there's a way to save ourselves some work, we'll find it."

The Forgiving Ghost

by C. B. Gilford

The murder – although Claude Crispin, the murderer, was the only one who knew that that's what it was – occurred in broad daylight, in bright sunshine. But not, of course, within view of any casual spectators. Nobody saw it; so everybody took it for what Claude Crispin said it was, an accident.

The first that any outsiders knew of it was when Claude Crispin raced his motorboat in from the center of the lake, and started shouting and waving his arms at the nearby joyriders and water skiers. He told them something about his wife's falling in the water and his not being able to find her.

Immediately, all the boats – some with their skiers still dangling behind them – raced for the spot. They found it when they found the swimming dog. Momo was the belligerent little Pekingese which had belonged to Mrs. Crispin. Claude babbled something to the searchers about how the dog had fallen into the water, and Mrs.

Crispin had jumped in to save her. Here was the dog still swimming, of course, but there was no sign of the mistress.

Somebody apparently thought that as long as they were there, they might as well save the dog. So Momo was pulled aboard one of the boats, where she showed her gratitude by shaking the water out of her fur rather indiscriminately and snarling at her rescuers. Claude looked especially askance at that part of the operation. Now that the Pekingese had provided the visible reason why Mrs. Crispin, a poor swimmer, had been in the water at all, he would really have preferred to let her drown.

Meanwhile, nearly all the other occupants of the boats had jumped into the water and were doing a lot of diving and splashing around. Claude, watching them, wrung his hands, wore an anguished expression, and generally gave the appearance of an anxious, worrying, tragic husband.

They were at it for some twenty minutes. But at the end of that time everyone was pretty well exhausted, and even the most enthusiastic divers were ready to admit that they weren't going to find Mrs. Crispin either dead or alive. When they related this fact to Claude, he burst into tears and started to shake so violently that a stranger had to climb into his boat and steer it back to shore for him.

Thereafter, it became an official matter. The sheriff was summoned and he came out to the lake with a couple of his deputies. Preparations got underway for a dragging operation. The sheriff himself, a kindly, sympathetic man, sat down with Claude and got the whole story from him.

Yes, the Crispins were city folks, Claude said, and they'd vacationed for several summers at this lake. One of their favorite pastimes had been to rent a motorboat and cruise aimlessly around. Claude was a pretty fair swimmer, though he didn't get much practice these days. Mrs. Crispin wasn't afraid of the water, but she'd been a very poor swimmer.

"Why didn't she wear a life jacket, like the rules say?" the sheriff demanded, but without too much harshness.

Claude shrugged his shoulders helplessly. "You know how women are," he answered. "My wife had a very good figure, looked fine in a bathing suit. So she was always interested in getting a tan. If she'd worn one of those jackets, it would have covered her up and she wouldn't have gotten the tan. So she just left the jacket in the bottom of the boat. Vanity, I guess you'd call it."

The sheriff nodded sagely. "And you say she jumped in on account of the dog?"

Claude let himself sound bitter. "She loved that dog as much as if it had been a kid. Took it with her everywhere. Don't ask me how the dog fell overboard, though. Usually my wife carried it around in her arms. But this time she was letting it ride up front by itself. I don't know whether it fell or jumped. The thing never seemed to have much sense. But there it was in the water suddenly, and my wife started screaming. Now, I'd have stopped the boat and jumped in after it myself, but my wife didn't wait even to ask me. The next thing I knew, she was gone, too. I slowed the boat down and did a U-turn, but by the time I got back to the place, my wife had already disappeared. I cut the motor and went in after her, but I never did see her. I don't know what happened. She was just gone."

The sheriff seemed to understand. "Sometimes," he said, "when a poor swimmer jumps into deep water, gets a cramp or something, he just sinks to the bottom and never does come up. I guess it was one of those cases."

And that was the verdict. Probably because the idea never once crossed his mind, the sheriff didn't even mention murder.

Though he'd gotten rid of his wife, Claude Crispin still had his wife's prized possession, Momo. Sometime later that same afternoon Momo's rescuer returned her to Claude, clean, dry, but in no better humor.

The instant the dog was brought into the one-room cottage, she began an immediate sniffing search for her mistress. When the mistress couldn't be found, she set up a mournful, yelping wail. Claude, alone now and able to vent his true feelings, aimed a kick which almost landed, and which was close enough to send the animal scurrying into a safe corner to cogitate upon what had gone wrong with the world.

"Alvina is dead," Claude explained happily and maliciously.

The dog blinked and stared.

"I guess for the moment," Claude went on, "I've got to endure you. I'm supposed to be so broken up about the accident that I've got to pretend that I'm cherishing you as my remembrance of my poor, dead wife. It won't last, though, I can promise you that. Your days are numbered."

Momo whined softly and seemed to be looking around for a route of escape.

Claude smiled. He felt good, very satisfied with himself. "Ought to be grateful to you, though, oughtn't I, Momo? You were a very convenient gimmick. But don't think that's going to do you any good once we're away from this place. You swim too well, Momo, so I won't try a lake on you. Some little something in your hamburger, maybe, and then you can fertilize my garden. As soon as we get home, Momo."

The dog cringed and lay down with her head between her paws. She'd endured unkind remarks from Claude before, and now the threat in his tone was unmistakable.

Claude lay back on the bed and closed his eyes. He had really and truly had a hard day. There'd been the strain and excitement of planning, the deed itself, and then the display of grief all afternoon. It had been rewarding, but quite wearing, too. He felt like sleep.

That was when the dog yelped. Claude had begun to drift off, and the noise woke him. Cursing, he sat up and looked toward the corner where he'd last seen Momo. The dog was still there, but not cringing any longer. Instead, Momo was standing up shakily on her hind legs, her tail wagging, her eyes shining. In fact, she was the very picture of canine ecstasy.

"Hello, Claude."

The voice was a familiar one. Alvina's voice. At first he was sure that he was either dreaming or imagining. He blinked his eyes, striving to come fully awake. But then he knew somehow that he was already awake, and he looked in the direction the dog was looking.

Alvina was standing there!

Not all wet and dripping, her hair tangled with seaweed. Not even in the bathing suit and bandana she'd last worn. This Alvina was quite dry, lipsticked and powdered, and in a gay little flowered frock he'd never even seen before. Her blue eyes were bright; her blonde hair was shining; and she stood just inside the door of the cottage, although Claude was quite sure that the door had neither opened nor closed.

"Claude, I said hello, and you haven't even answered me." Then she smiled, as if she'd suddenly remembered something. "Oh, of course. You're dreadfully surprised. You hadn't expected to see me ever again."

Claude stated the incredible. "You're alive!"

"Oh, no, Claude, I'm a ghost."

Instinctively he looked to Momo for confirmation. She wasn't, however, howling with fear as dogs are supposed to do in the presence of the supernatural. Instead, she was still wagging her tail, quite as if she too saw and recognized Alvina. But the strangest

60

fact of all was that, although Momo obviously was aware of the presence of her mistress, and would normally have run to Alvina to be picked up and petted, now she seemed to realize that this visitor was not the sort who could pick up and pet even the smallest dog. In other words, Claude reflected as he tried to sort out his thoughts – Momo knew it was Alvina and yet wasn't Alvina, a friendly spirit but a spirit nevertheless.

But Claude still found this hard to believe. "Are you sure you're a ghost? I mean . . ."

"Of course I'm a real ghost. I'd have to be, wouldn't I? I'm certainly not alive. Because you killed me. Remember, Claude?"

"It was an accident," he started to say automatically.

"Oh, for pity's sake, Claude," she interrupted him. "I should know, shouldn't I? I was there. It was murder. You pushed me in, dear, and then you held my head under water."

It wasn't till then that Claude began to wonder, not whether this was really Alvina's ghost, but more as to what Alvina's ghost was doing here. And with the curiosity came just a little tingle of fear.

"I swear to you, Alvina," he began again.

"Darling, I know it was murder, and

61

everybody where I came from knows it was murder. Only people who've been murdered get to come back as ghosts. Or didn't you know that?"

"No, I didn't know that," he admitted.

She threw back her head and laughed. It was Alvina's old laugh, tinkling and silvery. Momo barked in happy accompaniment to it. "Maybe you wouldn't have murdered me if you'd known that, eh, Claude?"

He decided he'd better be frank and honest. There wasn't much choice. "You are rather frightening," he said.

She crossed the room and sat down on the corner of the bed. Appropriately enough, he noticed, she seemed utterly weightless, and the corner didn't sag at all under her.

"Poor Claude," she said. "I didn't mean to frighten you. But as I said, murdered people do have the privilege of coming back, and I just couldn't resist the opportunity."

He was beginning to take little courage now from her mild manner. "Why did you come back, Alvina?"

"We parted so suddenly, dear. There wasn't time to discuss anything."

"What is there to discuss?"

"Well, Momo, for instance." At the mention of her name, the Pekingese wagged her tail. "Claude darling, I know you had reason to hate me, but I hope that feeling of yours doesn't extend to that innocent little dog."

Remembering his conversation with Momo of just a few minutes past, Claude felt himself blushing guiltily. "Momo really will never be happy with you gone, Alvina," he evaded.

"She can be happy if you'll try to make her happy. I know how you two have always been enemies, but it was your fault, Claude, not Momo's. Promise me you'll try to make friends with her. Promise me you'll take good care of her. She's an orphan now, you know, thanks to you. Will you promise me, Claude?"

Claude grabbed at the chance of getting off so easy. "I promise, I solemnly promise," he said.

"Thank you, Claude," she answered, and she seemed very sincere.

They sat in silence for a moment then. Alvina's ghostly eyes gazed on Claude almost affectionately. He tried to reciprocate, but found the situation a bit strained.

"Well, was that all you wanted?" he asked finally. "I mean, now that we've agreed about the dog, I suppose that puts your spirit at rest, Alvina, and now you'll be content to . . ."

He stopped, fumbling. What he wanted to say, of course, was that ghosts – even apparently friendly ones – made him nervous, and he'd prefer that she return to her watery grave and stay there. Saying it would have been impolite, however, and perhaps – he still wasn't sure of her attitude – a trifle dangerous.

"You've been very sweet, Claude," she said. "And I do feel a lot better now that I know Momo will be well taken care of. I'm so grateful to you."

If she was going to become so polite and sentimental and easy to get along with, he could afford to be decent himself. "Look, Alvina, I'm sorry..."

She leaned a little closer to him, and a little ghostly frown creased her brow. "Oh no, don't say that, darling. You have no reason to be sorry. I deserved what I got."

"You think so?" Surprise was building on surprise.

"I know so. I deserved to be murdered. I was simply an awful wife to you."

"Oh, I wouldn't say that, Alvina."

"But it's true. I'd become quite a witch. I didn't realize it when I was alive, but I see it all clearly now. I was selfish and headstrong and quarrelsome. I always wanted my own way, and I made a scene if

64

I didn't get it. And worst of all, I wasn't loving enough. Don't you completely agree on my little catalogue, dear?"

"Well, yes . . ."

"So you were quite justified in doing what you did, Claude. Isn't that so?"

"Alvina!"

"I mean it, Claude. I mean it absolutely. I deserved to get murdered."

"Well, now, I wouldn't go so far as to say that."

"It's the truth. So I want to tell you this, darling. And I mean it from the bottom of my heart. I forgive you completely."

He stared at her incredulously. There was a little tingling in him again. Not from incipient fear as before. From what then? He wasn't quite sure. But when someone is so generous and tolerant . . . well, it just gives one a funny feeling, that's all.

"Gee, Alvina . . ." he started to say.

But she was gone. Momo was whining piteously, and frantically running about the room from wall to wall, searching for something that was surely no longer there.

"Don't bring that dog in my apartment," Elise said. She was in purple toreador trousers today and stood with her hands on

65

her hips barring the passage. Her dark hair waved behind her as she shook her head.

"But, angel," Claude Crispin said, "it's my wife's dog."

"I know that," Elise snapped. "But I don't like dogs, and I liked your former wife even less."

"But, angel, I couldn't leave the dog at home alone. And I've got to take care of it."

"Why?" The electricity in Elise's dark eyes crackled. "Why don't you just get rid of it?"

"I promised..."

"You what?"

"Well, I sort of made a secret promise after my wife died. It was the least I could do. After all, I owed her something. Try to understand, angel. Don't be cruel. We have gained quite a bit, you know. There'll be no more interference. I'm free. Just the two of us..."

"Three," she corrected him. "You and me and the dog."

"But we're better off than before, aren't we? We've made progress. Please let me in, angel."

She hesitated for another long moment, scorning him with her eyes. Then, abruptly, she turned and walked away, leaving the passage free for him to enter. He slipped in,

66

bringing Momo on her leash, and closed the door behind him.

Gaining admittance didn't make Momo happy. She lay down just inside the door, watching Claude reproachfully, and making small glum sounds. But Claude ignored the dog, and followed Elise to the sofa, where he sat down close but without touching her.

"You took your sweet time coming to see me," Elise said viciously.

"Angel, I had to be discreet. I'm a widower. I'm supposed to be in mourning. I explained that to you."

"Three whole months. Did it have to be that long?"

"Maybe I was trying to be too cautious."

"You certainly were."

"Forgive me, angel." He put his arms out for her, but she squirmed away. "Won't you forgive me? I was torn between caution and passion, believe me, angel."

"And the caution won."

"All right. But it's over now. Let's make up for lost time."

"I'm afraid I'm not in the mood, Claude."

"Elise, I went through an awful lot for you. I took big chances. Seems you ought to forgive me a little caution in a case like this."

"I'll forgive you nothing. You'll have to

67

learn you can't toy with my affections this way, Claude Crispin. You can't leave me dangling for three whole months..."

Elise's bitter speech was interrupted suddenly by a sharp bark from Momo. Distracted, Claude looked at the dog. He found her sitting up, eyes bright, tail wagging. And Alvina was sitting in the chair opposite them.

"So this is the woman you murdered me for, Claude," she said.

"Alvina!" he breathed.

"Did you call me Alvina?" Elise demanded.

"Darling," Alvina explained, "she can't see me. So don't make her think you've gone crazy by talking to someone she doesn't know is here. I'll be very quiet. You just go ahead with what you were doing."

"Claude, what's the matter with you?" Elise wanted to know.

"Nothing. I'm just a little upset, I guess."

"She's very pretty, Claude," Alvina commented. "Much prettier than I was. Different type, too. More exciting and romantic."

"Look, Elise," Claude said, hastily rising from the sofa, "I think I'd better go home. I don't feel well."

68

"Go home? You just got here and I haven't seen you for three months."

Alvina sighed audibly. "She's the demanding sort, isn't she, Claude? I guess that makes women more desirable. I wish I could have been more that way."

"Elise." Claude was confusedly fumbling now. "Maybe some other time . . ."

"Claude, you stay here, or it's all over with us."

"But you don't want me, Elise. You're angry with me."

"You're so right. And I'm going to keep on being angry with you till you apologize."

"All right, I apologize."

"That's better."

"Am I forgiven then?"

"That will take some time. You'll have to make it up to me. I've sat around here waiting for you for three long months, and you'll have to make that up to me."

"She's very demanding, isn't she?" Alvina said. "Is that what makes her so interesting, Claude?"

"That doesn't make her interesting!" Claude shouted.

"Claude," Elise screamed, "don't shout at me! And besides, I don't know what you're talking about." Then she stood up, too, facing Claude angrily. "You don't show

69

up for three months. Then you come here without a decent explanation and you talk gibberish."

"Angel..."

"Don't angel me!"

"Is it presents you want, Elise? What can I do? Just tell me. I want to take up where we left off. I went through so much. You know what I did."

"I know nothing of the sort, Claude. Don't try to implicate me."

"But you're in it as much as I am."

"Oh no, I'm not. It was your idea, and you went through with it all alone."

"But you approved, angel. You wanted me to do it."

"Claude, if that's what you came here for, to tell me I'm just as guilty as you are, then you can leave."

Without waiting for him to accept her invitation, she turned from him and walked away, through the bedroom door, which she slammed behind her. Claude stood open-mouthed in the center of the living room, and Momo barked joyously.

"Poor girl," Alvina said, "she feels guilty. That's what's upsetting her so. I'm sure she's not like this normally, Claude, I want you to tell her that I've not only forgiven you, but I've forgiven her, too."

70

Claude sat down on the sofa again, heavily, wearily. "Thanks, Alvina. That's mighty decent of you."

"I'm sure the impression I just got of her is inaccurate."

"I'm afraid it isn't," Claude admitted with a frown. "She's headstrong. She's quarrelsome. She's tremendously selfish."

"But, darling, those are the very things that were wrong with me. Oh, I wish there was something I could do. The trouble is, you see, that ghosts can haunt only their murderers, and strictly speaking, Elise isn't even an accomplice. But I wish I could talk to her, and tell her everything I've learned. Because basically I think she must be a very nice girl. When are you going to get married, Claude?"

"Married?" The word startled him somehow.

"You did intend to marry her, didn't you?"

"Oh yes, she's always insisted on it. On her own terms, of course. The trouble is that now I don't know what her terms are."

"That makes her mysterious, darling. And mystery is so attractive."

"Look here, Alvina." He rose from the sofa again, greatly disturbed. "Are you trying to encourage me?"

71

"Darling," she remonstrated, "you went to an awful lot of trouble murdering me. I think you should get your reward. And if Elise is what you want, then I want her for you. You see, Claude, I still have your interests at heart. And, well, I must confess..."

"What, Alvina?"

"A little soft spot, I guess you'd call it."

"Really? That's very generous of you."

"Oh, no, it's still selfish, I'm afraid," she answered softly. "Sometimes, Claude, I have the very selfish yearning for another chance. If I could just get another body or something and come back to you, I'm sure I could do a much better job of making you happy than I did before."

He felt terribly embarrassed, felt he ought to do something or say something but he didn't know what. Poor Alvina...but he didn't want to say that.

She was gazing tenderly up at him. "Oh darn," she said, "I'm afraid I'm going to cry. Goodbye, darling. Good luck, too."

Then once again, and as suddenly as before, she was gone. Momo began to whine pitifully and lonesomely. And Claude Crispin felt pretty much the same.

Alvina was home waiting for him, when he returned from one of his many unsatisfactory visits to Elise's apartment. He'd left Elise in a rage, but here was Alvina placidly curled up in her favorite old chair and giving him a smile of welcome. He felt almost glad to see her. It had been over two weeks.

"How's Elise, darling? I didn't want to be a busybody and poke my nose in there, but I am concerned."

"Well, she still can't stand the dog."

Momo barked in confirmation.

"And even though I've gone to see her every day since, she still hasn't forgiven me for staying away for three months."

"Darling, she's just as unreasonable as I was, isn't she? That's too bad. I wish you could find someone more suitable. You know, it's too bad you can't murder Elise. Then she'd learn her lesson like I have." She paused, crestfallen. "Oh darn, that wouldn't work either, would it? The dead and the living can't get together very well."

He crossed the room and sat down on the hassock in front of Alvina's chair. Momo followed him and hopped up onto his lap. He petted the dog.

"You know something, Alvina?" he said. "If murder were the proper way of managing a woman, I wouldn't have to bother with

Elise at all. Because I would have already found the perfect woman in you."

"That's sweet of you, Claude." Her smile was radiant. "Isn't it too bad that things have to work out this way? That we couldn't reach our perfect understanding until it was too late? Oh, I wish there were some way. I've asked about borrowing another body somewhere, but they say it can't be done."

"Yes, I wish there were some way, too, Alvina," he said.

Momo agreed, barking enthusiastically.

"You know," Claude said suddenly, "I've just had a happy thought."

"What, darling?" Alvina's ghostly eyes lighted with hope.

"Well, though you can't join me, I could join you."

"Claude!"

"Yes, it's rather drastic, I know."

"What about Elise?"

"I don't think she'd mourn more than a day or two."

"But there are other things to consider, too. You're still a young man, Claude. You have so much to live for."

"What? Just tell me what? I lost everything when I lost you."

"Claude, darling. Oh, I wish I could kiss you."

74

"Can't you? Have you really tried?"

"I know I can't. I've been told. There's a barrier between us."

"Then if you can't cross it, I certainly shall!"

"Oh, Claude, do you mean it?"

"Of course I mean it. There must be something appropriate in that medicine cabinet. I'd go up to that lake again and use it, darling, for sentimental reasons. But that would mean an awful delay. And I'm impatient to be with you again."

"Claude, dearest . . ."

He stood up. "I'll go see what's in the medicine cabinet right now."

He rushed off, but her voice stopped him. He turned back.

"Claude, get something for Momo, too, will you?"

"Certainly. I don't want to be separated from Momo, darling, any more than I want to be separated from you."

When they met on the other side, Momo jumped down from Claude's arms and went running to Alvina. She leaped into her mistress's arms and cuddled there, giving off small, ecstatic squeaks.

"That's a lucky dog," Claude said. "When do I get my welcome kiss?"

75

But for the moment, Alvina and Momo were lost in the contemplation of each other, hugging and squealing and kissing. Claude was patient. He spent the time glancing around at his new surroundings.

"I never thought to ask you, darling," he said, "but what kind of place is this anyway?"

What prompted the question was the fact that a couple of strangers were approaching. They were wearing a sort of uniform, like doormen, or perhaps guards. The uniforms had a red and black motif.

"Claude Crispin?" one of them asked.

"That's me," Claude said.

"Come with us, Mr. Crispin."

"I'm afraid you don't understand," Claude objected. "This is my wife here. I intend to stay with her."

It was Alvina who explained the difficulty. "Claude darling, Momo and I really would like to have you stay with us. But there are those old rules, darling. You're a murderer, you know. You'll have to go to the other place."

And Alvina and Momo went back to hugging and kissing.

The Crazy

by Pauline C. Smith

Mrs. Sedonia Naughton, his stepmother, did not introduce him to her guest. She simply threw open his door and the two women stood there observing him as if he were a disturbingly unique but harmless animal in a zoo.

He seemed to be constructing something on a long, bare wooden table placed in the center of the many-windowed room. The room, while crowded, still gave the appearance of studied organization. Exquisitely executed sailboats floated within narrow-necked bottles, precision-model automobiles rode the shelves; oil paintings, water-colors, grotesquely beautiful masks climbed the walls between windows, and booklined cases rose to the ceiling; a restive room at rest only upon the corner bedstead, pristine and smooth, but with two bed pillows alertly vigilant at its head.

He acknowledged the presence of the women by raising smoky eyes for only an instant, then he returned to his work. With a probing forefinger, he rolled invisible tools on the bare table. Selecting one, he picked it up delicately, scrutinized it attentively; then, bending with absorption over the table, he used it with finical exaction upon a nonexistent object.

The women stood there for some minutes watching this extraordinary pantomime, which was conducted with such scrupulous authenticity that the guest leaned forward, slanted from the hips, squinting tiny eyes in an endeavor to see that which could not be seen. She caught herself in the act and straightened indignantly when he looked up for a moment, his eyes filled with derisive amusement.

Sedonia tapped her shoulder, drew her back into the hall, closed the door to his room and the two went on downstairs.

"Well, I never," gasped the visitor, safe once more in the living room. She sank to a chair, breathed heavily, and fanning herself with a limp hand, gasped again. "In all my born days, I never!"

Sedonia was satisfied. She smoothed her armored hips with small, soft, well-manicured hands, sat down, and poured.

The visitor took a sip of coffee, which seemed to revive her. Patting her lips daintily, she asked politely, "What is he making?"

"What is he *making?*" cried Sedonia. "Well, for heaven's sake, he's not making anything. I mean, not anything except a fool of himself." Sedonia was annoyed because her guest had not stated an obvious fact. So she stated it herself. "He's crazy, of course. He's been fiddling around with nothing on that bare table of his ever since his father died. Six months now!"

"My goodness. Maybe he *thinks* there's something there," observed her guest.

"Of course he thinks there's something there. He's crazy."

The guest leaned forward and dropped her voice to a whisper. "Have you ever looked?"

"*Looked?*"

"I mean, gone in and felt around . . ."

"On the *table?* Oh, for heaven's sake, of course not. Anyway, I never go in there. I don't clean in there or make the bed or anything. He does that. He wants it that way. His father told me so. Well, that's all right." She shrugged. "That's fine with me."

"Maybe it was his father's death that –"

"That made him crazy? No, it just changed his craziness. Before that, he used to break out of his shell once in a while. Oh, not much and not with me, but with his

79

father. His father'd go in his room and they'd talk up a storm, all about what he was making on that table, and he really made things then. He made all those models and painted the pictures and stuff.''

"Well, my stars!" said the guest.

"When I used to tell his father I thought he was crazy, he'd say no he wasn't, he was a warped genius, or an unconventional artisan, or if he was crazy, he was an idiot savant, whatever that is, and laugh.''

The visitor clucked a sympathetic tongue. Then she said, "He certainly doesn't look crazy.''

"No, I suppose he doesn't. He looks like his mother. There's a picture of her around here somewhere. She died when he was twelve or thirteen, that's ten – eleven years ago. . . .''

"Maybe it was her dying that made him –''

"All I know is he never went to school. From the very first, he never went to school, and you know they make kids go to school unless they're either dumb or crazy. You know that.''

Her guest nodded.

"Well, he's not dumb because he reads all those heavy books in there, and besides, he keeps getting new ones. And his father said he wasn't crazy because he had tutors for him all those years – teachers that came to the house – and he said he learned more than the tutors could teach him. But I still say he's crazy because he acts crazy."

Sedonia retreated into a short brooding silence, during which her guest tried not to clink her coffee cup nor to become obtrusive as she surreptitiously slid curious eyes about the room.

"I thought somebody ought to see him," Sedonia said, startling her guest. "I just thought somebody ought to see how crazy he acts, somebody who wasn't hand in glove with him and his father and the will. Somebody who'd say, 'He's crazy,' – somebody like you."

The guest, on cue, eager to please, answered, "He certainly *seems* to be crazy, working like that on something that isn't even there. He certainly does seem to be *some* kind of crazy, anyway," she repeated thoughtfully, remembering the mathematical precision of the busily skillful fingers, the frowningly intelligent face so keenly intent upon an invention that only he could touch and see.

"Well, sure he is," announced Sedonia. "I told his father he was crazy . . . that was a while after we were married, of course, and I came to this house. Oh, this house!" With

81

a crimson-tipped gesture of contempt, she waved away not only the lush Victorian elegance, but her guest's timid interjection as to its grandeur.

"After three years in it, I can't breathe any more. I thought, when we got married, with him retired and all, he'd take me places – to Mexico, Canada, England, France. Around the world even. Wouldn't you think –?" She withdrew once more into sullen refuge to dwell upon a cosmopolitan future she had been sure would be hers.... "Well, he wouldn't budge. He was older than I. Oh, much older," she said, fluffing unbelievably golden hair, "set in his ways, I suppose. And all hung up on his crazy son. Wouldn't leave him for a minute. 'So you won't leave him,' I yelled; 'that proves he's crazy and you're scared to go away.' Then he died and went away after all."

"What did he die of?" asked her guest.

"He fell down the steps." Sedonia pointed toward the steep, open stairway in the hall. "Right down those steps. I was watching from the top, and he hit each post and didn't move a muscle after he landed. So he died right away. The doctor said it was a heart attack."

"Tch tch," observed her guest.

"I never saw *him,* " she said as she pointed
82

at the ceiling, "move so fast. He was out of his room in nothing flat, pushed me away and leaped down the steps three at a time. But did he call the doctor or do any of the things a sane person would do, like see if his heart was beating or feel his pulse? No way. He just sat there on the floor in the hall by his father's body and looked up at *me* at the top of the stairs! At me, not his father! So I went and called the doctor from the upstairs phone. And I didn't go down until the doctor got here. Then I *had* to go down to let him in because *he*," again pointing at the ceiling, "wouldn't budge. Just sat there on the floor, not moving except for his head, his eyes on me every second, as I went around the body and walked to the door to let the doctor in the house. Even when he helped carry the body in to the sofa and all the while the doctor examined him, those eyes were on me, not on his father, the doctor, or anything else . . . and it was like that all during the funeral, too. . . ."

The guest shuddered.

"Well, I was scared enough to tell the doctor about it, and the doctor said oh, pooh, pooh, that he'd known him all his life and, being a pundit, whatever that is, he'd probably react that way during shock and didn't even know what his eyes were looking at."

83

"My, my," breathed the guest.

"Then, after the funeral, he kept his eyes on me all the time the lawyer read the will. And as soon as the will was read, he got up and went upstairs and closed his door, and that's when I told the lawyer how he watched me all the time and how crazy he was and that I was afraid he'd go violent any minute. The lawyer said something about ah, no, he wasn't crazy or violent or any of those things, he was a sophist, whatever a sophist is. Then he patted me on the shoulder and told me not to worry, that I was now comfortably well off as long as I sat tight and let *him* –" pointing at the ceiling "– do his own thing."

"Well!" said the guest.

"At least one thing. Right after that, he got all wrapped up in that nothing on his table and he hasn't looked at me since."

"That's one thing," agreed the guest.

"But the will won't be probated for a year – well, six months now."

"What's probated?" asked the guest.

"It means everything will be legally mine. The money, house, and *him*," nudging her shoulder ceilingward. "That's the way the will goes. Like I'm kind of his keeper. So I said to the lawyer, 'If I'm his keeper, it means he's crazy. Right?' 'Wrong,' said the lawyer, 'it means you're a mentor,' whatever that is."

"Goodness!" said the guest.

"And it means I'm stuck in this house, with enough money to travel anywhere..."

"That's wonderful!" cried the guest.

"But I can't go. Not, at least, until the will is probated."

Sedonia leaned forward and poured a fresh cup of coffee for her guest, who gulped it down in one swallow, and asked, "Yes?" with a gasp.

"Well, you see," said Sedonia in a tone of confidence, "once that will is probated, it means I can *do* something."

"What?" asked the guest.

"It means I can get somebody in here – a doctor who is not hung up on pundits and a lawyer who hasn't got a sophist routine, and have these new ones, who aren't hand in glove with the family, look over that crazy you-know-who," as she pointed on high, "and I bet I can get him committed in nothing flat."

The guest clapped her hands.

"Because he's crazy. You saw how he is."

"My goodness, yes," affirmed the guest, remembering the derisive smile and smiling now in happy retaliation.

Sedonia sat back in her chair and folded

her arms across stiffly ample breasts. "Then," she said, "once I get him put away, maybe I can sell this house and live a little."

Sedonia moved into her slim and golden, youthful, exciting cosmopolitan world of fancy, and the guest sensed the visit to be over.

She rose with a vague murmur as to duties involving grandchildren home from school and thought, momentarily, as she rose, of the crazy young man upstairs; entertaining a flash of comprehension that he might be – he just might be – working on something with true substance, something real.... "Well," she said, and moved across the flowers of the carpet.

Sedonia ushered her out the door, promising brightly, "We'll see each other again.... On the park bench sometime?"

"Oh my, yes," agreed the guest. She started down the broad cement steps, then turned as the door began to close. "You know," she offered timidly, "maybe you ought to feel around on that table – just feel around, you know ..." but the door was now shut and she walked across the park toward the reality of a cramped apartment, swarming with hungry, disrespectful grandchildren whom she must feed and suffer, and wished she lived back there in the old house on this side of the park with a crazy stepson bent studiously over a bare table. . . . One thing, though, if she did, she most certainly would feel around on that table to learn, to really learn, if there was something there.

Sedonia felt the vindication of proof. Someone else, a stranger, an unbiased outsider, one without ties or guilt, had attested to the craziness of her stepson.

After pouring herself a half cup of fresh coffee, she walked to the kitchen and filled the cup with brandy. Then she climbed the stairs, unconsciously avoiding the banister side down which her late husband had toppled, striking every post of each tread along the way.

She reached the hall above, turned, and opened the door of her stepson's room. She stood there, sipping her coffee and brandy, watching him.

He appeared to pick up something from the table and wind it around something else.

Sedonia shook her head, smiled, and took a drink of coffee.

He crouched, squinted through a nothing-object along the top of the table, then he drew back his arm, inserted what he thought he had into what he thought he was looking through and rammed it back and forth, with vigor yet with delicacy and a certain grace.

Sedonia continued to sip her coffee.

He was in no hurry. He withdrew what he was using, unwound whatever had been around it, and laid the two on the bare table. Then he bent over, snapped his thumb, picked up something from the apparently bare table with his left hand and plucked, with his right thumb and forefinger, from the palm of his left hand, six small nonexistent objects, dropping them, one by one, into a nonexistent receptacle.

Sedonia drooped skeptical lips, leaned against the side of the doorway, and sipped her coffee.

He pressed something shut with his thumb and cocked another open with his forefinger. He picked up one object in empty arms. He swung around then, looking at and through Sedonia.

She lounged against the doorframe, languidly sipping coffee, whispering, "Crazy," through the liquid.

He raised his cradled arms and seemed to adjust a featherweight. His left hand curved emptily before him, his right grasped air alongside his hunched shoulder, and the right forefinger, stiffly outright, curled slowly and with purpose.

He moved his head an infinitesimal distance, closed his left eye, squinted his right, and the forefinger closed in.

Sedonia jerked, the cup and saucer sounding a velvet clatter against the carpet, her fool's-gold hair blowing gently. She crumpled in slow motion, sliding softly down the doorjamb while she faced the forefinger that stiffened and closed five more times before she reached the flowers of the floor.

He laid the cradled object down on the bare table. Then he watched, but did not move toward, Sedonia's body that showed no mark of violence and finally settled peacefully.

He bent over the table and, with quick flicks of his fingers, pushed unobservable and no longer needed tools aside into a small invisible pile. He walked to a window and opened it wide, returned to the table, bent his knees, and swept them all into his arms. He took them to the window, heaved them forth onto the shrubbery below.

He closed the window, glanced impassively at Sedonia on his doorsill, crossed the room, stepped over her body and to the phone in the upper hallway.

He dialed the doctor, and then the lawyer, explaining in his pundit voice, with sophist phraseology, that his erstwhile stepmother, wife of his murdered father, was now dead of a heart attack, probably caused by virulent imagination.

He hung up the phone, crossed the hall, stepped over dead Sedonia, and deliberated at his bare table before lifting something from it. He held the object lightly in a curved hand and walked with it toward his bed in the corner.

There, he lifted the top bed pillow and laid the object gently on the other where one might imagine a vaguely outlined indentation of a shotgun, stock and barrel hazily defined on the soft, white surface.

He placed the top bed pillow over the hiding place and smoothed it with care.

Police Calls

by Carroll Mayers

I am rather agitated when I phone police headquarters that first evening, but the officer I draw certainly is not. "What was that address again, Mr. Waters?"

"Walters. The Creston Arms. Apartment 4D."

"And this man in the hall, he was trying to open your apartment door?"

"That's what it looked like," I say. "He was picking at the lock with something –"

"Just like on TV, huh?"

"I don't see what –"

"No offense, sir. Can you give a description of the guy?"

"Nothing definite," I say. "He spun around, ran down the fire stairs when I yelled."

"That wasn't very smart, Mr. Waters."

"Look –"

"I mean, you should've quietly backed away, called us from another phone. He could've gotten violent."

I draw a breath. "So I didn't think," I say. "I was startled, just coming off the elevator –"

"Yeah...well, that's water over the dam," he says philosophically. "Anything special you'd like us to do?"

I blink, wondering if I am hearing okay. "I beg pardon?"

"I've made a record. Glen Waters. The Creston Arms. Apartment 4B."

"Walters. 4D."

"Oh. Thanks. Like I say, I've got it all down..."

"And you're not going to do anything about it?"

He is very patient. "You've got to understand, Mr. Walters," he explains. "This's a busy department, we can't hightail all over town on every petty sneak-thief call. Especially with no specific description..."

I sigh again. "Thank you, officer," I say. "I only thought I should call." And I hang up, trusting I will never have to call again.

But I do, three nights later. The voice which takes my call tells me it is the same officer. I am not enthusiastic.

"This is Glen Walters at the Creston Arms, Apartment 4D," I say. "I want to report a break-in."

"Yes, sir."

92

"There was a man in my apartment when I came back from visiting down the hall –"

"What time was this, Mr. Waters?"

"Walters. Just now; only a couple of minutes ago. As I said, when I came back –"

"Just a second, sir. You say Walters. Didn't you call in a few nights back? Something about a guy picking your lock?"

I am conscious my chest is beginning to tighten. "That's correct," I say. "It appears burglars are getting to consider my apartment some kind of windfall, but I can't help that –"

"Mr. Walters, do you realize how many crank calls this department gets in a week?"

I control myself admirably. "This is not a crank call, officer," I say stiffly. "My other contact was not a crank call. I am only reporting an attempted robbery –"

"No offense intended, sir. I only want you to appreciate our position."

"And I'm trying to make you appreciate mine," I say. "There was a man in my apartment when I got back to it. I surprised him in the living room. He must've only just gotten in because nothing was disturbed yet. When he heard me behind him –"

"How had he gotten in, Mr. Walters? I mean, were there marks on the doorjamb?

Maybe you've heard: they're called jimmy marks, professionally."

A buzzing in my head begins to complement the constriction in my chest. "I didn't notice any," I tell him. "Probably I didn't fully close the apartment door when I left, and the latch didn't catch."

"Why had you gone down the hall, Mr. Walters?"

"Dammit, officer, what difference does that make?"

"Only for the record, sir."

The buzzing is stronger now. "Well, for the record," I say distinctly, "I had gone down to visit a new tenant to borrow a cup of sugar."

"Aha!" he chuckles into the phone. "The old cup of sugar dodge, huh? What is she, Mr. Walters, a blonde? Or a redhead?"

(In fact, the lady in question is neither, being a most toothsome brunette with whom I am very anxious to become acquainted on – ah – intimate terms. The acquisition of and involvement with such luscious fillies is a particular hobby of mine. Unfortunately, in this instance my bright smiles and nods in lobby and elevator are being pointedly ignored, and tonight my sugar ploy has fallen flat.)

94

I lace sarcasm into my rejoinder. "For the record, I assume?"

His chuckling dies a bit. "Sorry, sir. You know how it is, a little levity now and then. So – what happened when you surprised your intruder?"

"He whirled, swung at me, and knocked me down," I say simply. "By the time I'd regained my feet, he'd bolted out the door and was gone."

"You get a good look at him?"

"No. Chunky. Dark features. Dark sweater and slacks. That's about all."

"He get away with anything?"

"I don't think so," I say. "I haven't made a thorough check, but I believe I came back sooner than he'd expected. I imagine he's been watching various apartments, mine included, and when he saw me step out and the door didn't latch, he grabbed the opportunity."

"Most likely," he agrees. "We get a lot of squeals like that. Well, anything special you'd like us to do?"

I close my eyes. Counting to one hundred would have been silly, but I do make it to ten. Then I say deliberately, "You asked me that the other time."

He's contrite. "I probably did, Mr. Waters, but –"

"Walters, dammit!"

"Sorry. But you've got to understand –"

What with my tight chest and buzzing head, I guess I am truly agitated now. "I know," I cut in. "I can't give you any good description; and the man likely didn't take anything anyhow; and I can't expect you to be chasing around town – so let's forget the whole thing." And I hang up.

When I have to call the police once more the following week, I make up my mind there will be no nonsense if a certain officer happens to draw my "squeal." He does, and there isn't.

"This is Glen Walters again," I tell him firmly. "The Creston Arms. Apartment 4D. I have been out for the evening and have just returned. I went to the movies. It's now eleven thirty-two. The bedroom window of my apartment, on the fire escape, has been broken open; I can see the jimmy marks. There was no money on the premises, but the rooms have been ransacked. I want you to send someone over here right away –"

"No money loss, you say, Mr. Walters?"

"Dammit, man, that's not the point."

"We're awful busy tonight. There's a Shriners' convention and the traffic problem's something fierce –"

Chest, head, the works are starting up

again. I almost yell into the phone. "Don't you understand?" I plead. "Thieves keep breaking into this apartment! I demand an investigation."

"But –"

"No buts, officer! I want a detective over here. I want him over here immediately." This time, when I hang up, I hope it rattles his teeth.

For all my belligerence, I am not actually holding my breath waiting for said detective. It is just as well; nobody ever comes. I guess my citing no actual financial loss has something to do with it. That, and maybe the fact that there is a considerable number of Shriners in the country.

In any event, all the foregoing is a preamble to tonight. I am in quite an anticipatory state because the schedule calls for the company of a delectable redhead named Felicity (propitious omen?) I happened to meet in an intimate singles bar the evening before. Under my subtle blandishments, luscious Felicity has agreed to visit me tonight for cool cocktails, warm stereo, and whatever. Thought of the whatever is especially enthralling; the unexpected smooch Felicity bestowed on me in the bar promises much.

She is due shortly after eight. I have a few

errands about town, but I get back to the apartment at seven thirty. And walk in on disaster. Once again the rooms have been ransacked – plus.

Naturally, I am sick; my evening is zilch. But I am not too sick to formulate my impending call to the authorities. This time there will be no yelling, no cursing – and no putoffs.

Accordingly, when I phone I am restrained but emphatic. My luck being what it is, I get the same officer, but even this does not deter me. I review all the pertinent facts crisply and then I conclude. "This is my fourth call in the past two weeks. I admit I suffered no previous losses, probably because those thieves were primarily interested in cash and I keep no loose cash on hand –"

"I should've told you before, sir. If they're looking just for money, it's likely amateurs. The professionals, you understand, will take anything . . ."

"I do understand," I say coldly, "and this time they did. A clock radio is missing, and two suits of clothes, and a portable TV –"

"Say, that's a shame! Was it a color TV?"

"– and a set of gold cufflinks. Now *you* understand something, officer. I definitely, positively expect a police investigation this time. I expect a detective – a real live, flesh-

and-blood detective – to come here tonight. Within the hour. Failing that, I'll go to the city commission. I'll go to the mayor. I'll go to the governor."

"I can appreciate how upset and all you are, Mr. Waters, but –"

He is talking into a dead phone because, my resolution holding, I quietly break the connection. I am confident that my firm ultimatum will at last result in official action.

In the meantime, though, my exhilarating evening is ruined. I begin to half-straighten up the apartment, then reflect I should leave everything for the detective to witness. It also occurs to me to telephone Felicity (we'd exchanged numbers at the bar) to temporarily cancel her visitation. I try to reach her but nobody answers; unfortunately, she's probably already under way. Well, she'll understand. . . .

The detective who comes is lean and tired-looking, with mournful brown eyes like a beagle's. He stands in the middle of the living room, looks around, and shakes his head.

"It's a mess all right, Mr. Waters. You wonder how they know, eh?"

"Walters. Know what?"

"Where's a good place to hit. You take my

aunt, over in Capitol City. She was hit just the past month. Lot of valuable antiques."

"This isn't the first time," I tell him grimly. "Counting tonight, I've called you people four times."

He shakes his head again. "Is that a fact? But then, I guess you've got insurance?"

My chest twinges. I say, "Look, officer –" and then I break off as the door buzzer echoes. I move to answer, expecting it will be Felicity.

It is. She stops in the doorway with a bright, tantalizing smile on her wet lips, and then she tilts forward from her spike heels and gives me a big kiss. "Hi, lover boy!"

I am a trifle embarrassed under the circumstances, but I assume the detective is a man of the world. I start to usher Felicity inside and then I stop, principally because said detective is abruptly making funny noises.

I swing back, surprised. The detective is looking – no, glaring – at Felicity, and now he is mouthing words. "So," he tells her furiously, "my ever-loving wife really gets around, doesn't she? I've been suspecting as much!"

After that, the action gets hectic as the detective's tired blood perks up miraculously and he closes in on me, smashes my nose, knocks out two teeth, blacks one eye. Through it all, I vaguely appreciate you don't have to be single to patronize a singles bar. I also deplore footloose wives, particularly when they're married to cops. . . .

So be a good citizen. Curb your dog, don't litter the sidewalk, and obey traffic regulations. But be a bit hesitant about calling the police, demanding action. Eventually, you just might get the wrong kind.

For myself, I plan two steps as soon as they release me from this hospital:

First, I'll move to another apartment – with triple locks.

Then I'll have the phone disconnected.

Funeral in a Small Town

by Stephen Wasylyk

Barrett drove grimly, the speedometer needle well above sixty-five until he left the turnpike and headed east on the Fox River Road, a twisting, turning blacktop through the mountains that still held patches of ice and snow where the tall pines had blocked out the sun.

There was no sun this morning. The sky was gray and low, like the mood that had settled on Barrett when the phone had rung in the cool darkness of his bedroom long before dawn.

"Page," his Aunt Edna had said softly, "you'll have to come up here. Lou is dead."

The question stuck in Barrett's throat. "How?"

He sensed from the silence that his aunt didn't want to put it into words, as if not saying it would make it not true. "Killed," she said finally. "Someone went into the newspaper office last night and shot him."

102

Barrett let the words sink in, not wanting to believe them any more than she did.

"I'll be there," he said. "As fast as I can make it."

He flicked on the lamp between the twin beds, to be confronted by the annoyance in his wife's eyes as she blinked away the sudden brilliance. Phone calls at odd hours were nothing new for Barrett, but Deb had never become used to or accepted them. It was only one of the points of friction between them lately. It wasn't the major one.

For months, his aunt and uncle had been asking him to come back to the small town in the mountains where he had been born, where his uncle was the editor and publisher of the small weekly newspaper, so that his uncle could retire and turn the paper over to Barrett. Barrett, feeling hemmed in by the city and wanting to turn back the pages of his life to what he knew was a more free, unhurried existence, was in favor of the move, but his wife had announced firmly she had no intention of living in a small town.

His wife brushed back her long blonde hair. "Another crisis at the agency?"

"Far more serious," Barrett said. "Lou was killed last night."

She swung out of bed and into a robe in one fluid motion, a graceful woman almost

103

as tall as Barrett, with a slim, well-proportioned body that never failed to stir him, even now. She accepted the announcement without shock or curiosity, which didn't surprise Barrett. As long as his uncle was alive, the decision to move or not to move could be postponed indefinitely. Now that he was dead, the decision would have to be made soon, and that was uppermost in her mind. "I assume you are going up there?"

He nodded. "You'll come with me, of course."

"No," she said. "He was your uncle, not mine."

Barrett felt a familiar touch of frustration and anger. There were times when he didn't understand her, couldn't understand her. "It would only be common courtesy."

"No," she said again. "I won't go. I have always felt out of place there." There was an inflection in her voice that said if he wanted to argue, she was prepared.

Not this time, Page Barrett thought wearily. *There are more important things to do.* He dialed Elmdorf, who headed the advertising agency where Barrett was a well-paid account executive, and explained the situation to him.

"Take as much time as you like," Elmdorf had said. "We'll talk when you get back."

Barrett knew what he meant. Elmdorf was aware of his uncle's offer and sided with Barrett's wife in thinking he should turn it down. His reasons were as self-centered as hers. Barrett controlled a large amount of business that the agency would probably lose if he left.

A patch of ice forced Barrett's thoughts to the immediate present. The car started to skid and Barrett twisted the wheel sharply and then he was back on the roadway, topping a small rise, a snow-covered valley spread before him. The Fox River bisected the whiteness like a piece of dark blue, twisted yarn, making a slight bend below, where a bridge took the road across and into a small town.

Barrett slowed. He always enjoyed this particular moment, summer or winter, when the valley unfolded suddenly and his long trip was almost ended.

A bright red VW, skis strapped to its rear deck, horn raucous, flashed by and cut back too quickly, forcing Barrett off the road and into the snow, inches away from the guard barrier and the long steep slope to the river. Barrett fought the car back onto the road and stopped. He took a deep

105

breath. If he had been going just a little faster . . .

He looked down the slope. Except for a few scattered trees, there was nothing to have kept him from tumbling into the river.

He curbed an impulse to take out after the VW, but the little car was already halfway to the bridge, a small red speck speeding down the curving roadway. If it belongs around here, we'll meet again, Barrett reflected grimly as he set the car in motion.

Fox River looked no different from usual when he drove through, and Barrett was conscious of a slight surprise. He didn't know exactly what he had expected from the town because his uncle had been killed, but business as usual wasn't part of it, not with his uncle's position in the community.

Lou Beck and his newspaper had been the guiding light and the conscience of Fox River and the surrounding county for almost forty years, ever since he woke one morning tired of the push and the odor of the big city and the pressure of working for a metropolitan daily. Within a week he and Edna Beck had been headed for his home town, his bank savings in his pocket after a phone call had confirmed the weekly was for sale.

He had grown old there, surrounded by the dusty, dry smell of the newspaper office,

106

of printing ink and hot lead, of the oil-soaked old press in the back room. He had made Barrett his reporter at sixteen, during high school summer vacation, hammering at his copy until Barrett knew what he meant when he said, "Write the facts, boy, and keep it short. Opinions are for the editorial page and I write that. You stay at it long enough and I'll make you a good newspaperman."

Barrett smiled, remembering his uncle's disapproval when he had gone into advertising. His opinion had been expressed in one healthy snort of disgust and he thereafter referred to Barrett's work only as that job of yours."

Barrett swung the car into his aunt's driveway. Waiting and watching for him, she opened the door, her silver hair neatly set, her small figure erect and already dressed in black, her arms outstretched, and Barrett had the feeling he had come home after a long absence.

Sometime later, he curled his fingers around a cup of coffee in the warm kitchen, examining the fine porcelain as if he were seeing it for the first time, wondering how to ask the questions that had to be asked. He sipped the coffee. "Tell me about it."

"I have very little to tell. Lou came home last night for dinner, took a short nap, and went back to the office. You know he always worked late the night before they started printing the paper. He was usually home by ten. At eleven, I called the office but there was no answer. I became worried, so I called Grant Rhodes and asked him to look into it."

Barrett nodded. Grant Rhodes was the chief of the three-man police force, and he and Lou had been friends for years.

"About an hour later, Grant came to the door. I knew something was wrong, but I never dreamed of anything like this. Grant said it looked like someone had just walked up behind Lou and shot him. Why, Page? Why should anyone shoot him?"

Barrett avoided the tear-filled eyes. "I don't know. All we can do now is try to find out. I'll go speak to Grant."

He slipped into his coat, knowing she hadn't asked yet why his wife wasn't with him, dreading the question because there was really no answer. She watched him affectionately, reaching out to turn up his coat collar. Barrett smiled. She had done that often when he was a boy, when he had come to live with them after his parents had died.

"Deb won't be coming?" she asked suddenly.

Embarrassed, Barrett shook his head.

"Well," said his aunt, "I suppose she has her reasons."

"You should have someone to stay with you," Barrett suggested.

"I do. Cindy Neal. You probably don't remember her. She was a little girl when you went off to college. She teaches English now at the high school and helped Lou at the paper with the women's pages. She's down at the office with Tom Cottrell."

Cottrell had been his uncle's combination typesetter, makeup man, and pressman, had been with the paper since the day Lou had bought it, and Barrett wondered what he would do now that the old man was dead.

"I'll stop by and see them," said Barrett.

He decided to walk. The town wasn't that big and, while it was cold, it wasn't the bitter dampness winter brought to the city. He found Grant Rhodes in his office, a thin man in a tan uniform, with a hook nose, skin that had the patina of well-cared-for leather, and a mouth bracketed by deep creases.

Rhodes motioned him to a chair. "I was expecting you, Page."

"Anything to tell me?"

"We are investigating, but we have very little to go on. Your uncle was alone in the office, sitting at his desk. Someone came up behind him and shot him in the back of the head with a small-caliber gun. There must be hundreds of those in the county, so we have nothing there. It had to be between nine, when Cottrell left as usual, and eleven, when I found him."

"Robbery?"

"In a town where people don't even lock their doors? His wallet was in his pocket. Nothing was missing from the office. Nothing there worth stealing, really."

"No motive at all?"

"None that is apparent. I can't think of one person who would want to kill Lou. To tell you the truth, Page, I'm a little out of my depth with this one, just as I was with the other."

Barrett sat a little straighter. "The other?"

"You wouldn't have heard about it in the city, but one of the local kids, a sixteen-year-old girl, was found raped and strangled in the woods about a week ago. The poor kid had been on the way home from school when someone caught her." He shook his head. "There is nothing yet on that one, either. Just some tracks in the snow that mean nothing. No one saw or heard anything." He sighed. "Peaceful county like this goes on for years with no trouble, then two killings within a week."

"Maybe there is a connection."

"The kind of man who would attack a young girl is not the same who would shoot an old man. At least, in my opinion."

Barrett nodded and rose. "I'll go over to the office and look around. Maybe I can find something that will help."

"If you need me, I'll be here." Rhodes pulled a long black cigar from his pocket and lit it, eyeing Barrett through the smoke. "I suppose you'll be taking over the paper now?"

Barrett shrugged and walked out. He had forgotten there were no personal affairs in this town.

He came across the red VW at the curb in front of the drugstore across the street from the newspaper office, the skis still in the rack. Lips tight, he walked around the car. Dents in the right side showed that his hadn't been the only car forced off the road.

Barrett entered the drugstore, eyes searching. Several young men and women dressed in ski clothes were seated at the soda fountain, others occupying the booths. It was impossible to tell which was the driver of the VW.

Behind the prescription counter at the rear of the store, a short, heavyset man with a bald head smiled and beckoned. He held out his hand as Barrett approached. "Glad to see

111

you back, Page. Sorry about Lou, but still good to see you again."

A widower, Allen Carey had been the town pharmacist for almost as long as Lou had owned the paper, and he was a good one. He filled prescriptions cheerfully, even in the small hours of the morning, and did a little emergency *sub rosa* prescribing on his own.

Barrett jerked a thumb over his shoulder. "I don't suppose you know who owns the red VW with the ski rack that's parked out front?"

"I certainly do. It belongs to my boy Pete. He's a real ski nut. Spends almost all his time over at the ski resort on Big Bear Mountain." He winked at Barrett. "Don't know how much skiing he gets done, though. I think he goes for the company more than anything else. What's wrong?"

"That car almost ran me off the road this morning," said Barrett.

"Pete did that? Are you sure?"

"You don't forget a car that color," said Barrett. "Where is he now?"

"Asleep. I told you he went for this *aprés ski* stuff. He was out all night." He winked at Barrett again. "You know a lot of these kids come up from the city to ski. Some of them are real lookers, too. I can't blame him.

Sometimes I wish I wasn't so old. Some of these young girls . . ."

Barrett felt a sense of distaste, as if Carey had said something obscene. "How old is he?"

"Turned twenty-one last summer."

"I thought he'd be in college."

Carey's eyes shifted, flicking around the store. "Well, he's not much interested in that. He helps me out occasionally."

Barrett didn't need it spelled out any further. The apologetic tone admitted that Pete Carey was a ski bum. Barrett decided to let the incident go. Carey had enough trouble. "Tell him to drive more carefully," he said. "I'll see you later."

"I guess you'll be around here a lot more, now that Lou is gone."

Barrett couldn't tell if that made Carey happy or not. "That remains to be seen," he said. Evidently there was no one in town who didn't expect him to take over the paper.

Carey, reaching for Barrett's hand, brushed a small prescription bottle from the counter. It splattered on the marble floor with a small crash. Carey grinned weakly. "Part of the profits gone."

Wondering if Carey became nervous every time he talked about his son, Barrett shook

113

his hand and stepped out into the cold afternoon.

The newspaper office was a former store, fronted with a plate glass window and a door tucked away in a little vestibule. The shades were drawn. Overhead, a sign in Old English lettering said: FOX RIVER TRIBUNE, LOU BECK, EDITOR-PUBLISHER. The sign was weather-beaten and old. *Like Lou*, thought Barrett.

He pushed the door open and stepped inside. A rail and a waist-high counter separated the office from the door, not enough of a barrier to keep the cold draft from reaching a young woman at a desk in the corner. She stood up.

She was dark-haired and tall, wearing a turtleneck jersey over a plaid skirt, white boots almost reaching her knees. Her nose was small and upturned, giving her a pleasantly aggressive look, and her eyes were widely spaced above a generous mouth. It was the kind of face that would wear well through the years, Barrett decided.

"I'm Page Barrett," he said, pushing his way through a swinging gate in the office itself. "You must be Cindy Neal."

She nodded. "We've been expecting you." She indicated the back room and Barrett was aware of the soft hum of a motor, the spaced

114

whump and the familiar staccato tinkle of brass mats dropping that told him someone was operating a Linotype machine. "Tom Cottrell is here."

Barrett wondered what Cottrell would be working on. He slipped off his coat and moved to the back room.

Cottrell looked up over the copy board and shifted a pipe from one side of his mouth to the other. "Page. Wondered when you'd get here."

"Working on the paper?" Barrett was puzzled. "I would think –"

"Figured Lou would want it this way. Paper is almost complete and would be a waste not to print it. I was thinking that if you showed up you could write a story about Lou. I can fit it in on page one by dropping something."

"That's what a good newspaperman would do," Barrett said dryly.

Cottrell removed the pipe and studied it. "Lou would do it. He'd expect you to do the same. The people in this county buy the paper to read the news and no matter how he died, Lou's death is news. You can't deny that."

"No," said Barrett. "I can't deny that, but I'm more interested in finding out who killed him and why. What do you know?"

"Nothing." He drew on the pipe reflectively. "Nothing you can ask me that I haven't already asked myself, Page, and I've got no answers."

He sat behind the Linotype machine, a thin, narrow-chested man dressed in blue work clothes, his sleeves rolled up on sinewy arms, metal-rimmed spectacles pushed up into his gray hair. Barrett was sure that Cottrell was working, not because he didn't care what had happened to Lou, but because he cared a great deal and preferred to keep busy rather than think about it.

"I guess I can still write a story," Barrett said gently. "Not as well as Lou, but good enough."

He stepped into the office. To his left were a half dozen steel filing cabinets; to his right a small heavy iron safe that Barrett knew held nothing but bookkeeping records. Along one wall was Cindy Neal's desk, and an ancient, massive typewriter on a wheeled stand flanked Lou Beck's rolltop desk and chair. Opposite the desk, a large drawing table held a pad of newspaper layout sheets that Lou used to guide Cottrell in making up the pages, filling in the blank columns with the ads and the stories as they developed. There would be a set of those for this issue in the back room and

116

Cottrell would require no help from Barrett there.

Rhodes had been right. There was absolutely nothing in the office worth stealing.

The top of the desk was raised, the pigeonholes exposed and filled with projecting papers, but the working area of the desk was clean. Barrett frowned. That was unusual. He could not recall a time when Lou did not have papers scattered about, limiting himself to a small area in which to work.

"Who cleaned the desk?" he asked Cindy.

"I don't know," she said. "It was like that when I came in early this morning. Instead of going to the high school, I went to your aunt's house. I stayed with her for a few hours before coming here."

"Lou was working at the desk when you left last night?"

"As usual. He had papers scattered –" She stopped, realizing what Barrett was implying. "They're gone," she said. "Whatever he was working on is gone. There were some photographs, too," she added circumspectly.

"Photographs?"

She nodded. "I didn't look at them but I know they were there."

Barrett picked up the phone. Automatic

dialing for Fox River was still a year away, and the operator's voice asked him for his number. "I want Chief Rhodes," he said.

He wasted no time when Rhodes answered. "Grant, did you clean off Lou's desk when you removed the body?"

There was a silence. "No," said Rhodes finally. "As near as I can remember, the desk was clean. You onto something?"

"I think I know what the killer took from the office."

"Something valuable?"

"I can't see how," said Barrett. "It was just a story and some photos." He cradled the phone gently, wondering what there could possibly be about a news item in a small town weekly that would be worth stealing.

Cindy Neal had moved closer to him and he caught the faint scent of an indefinable perfume. It was a pleasing scent, a bright, fresh fragrance very much different from anything his wife would wear.

"You have any idea of what Lou was writing?" he asked.

"Not exactly. I know he had been spending some time at the Big Bear Mountain Ski Resort. He'd been over there often the last few days."

"Do you know who he was seeing?"

"A man named Horn, I believe. You could talk to him."

He slipped into his coat. "I'll need my car."

She dangled keys before him. "No need. We'll take mine."

Barrett couldn't say no. He had to admit he would enjoy her company.

She made the thirty miles to Big Bear Mountain in a half hour, handling the car expertly, downshifting smoothly on the occasionally slippery road without losing speed. The ski resort was off the main highway on a back road that seemed to wind halfway around the mountain. Before they pulled into the parking lot, Barrett could see the two chair lifts operating to capacity, carrying brightly dressed skiers to the top of the long slopes.

The lodge at the foot of the chair lifts was low and rambling, bigger than Barrett remembered, and he realized that several additions had been built since he had last been here. They found Horn in a walnut-paneled office, a pale gnome of a man wearing ski boots and casual clothes that Barrett would have bet had never seen a ski slope.

"I'm sorry to hear about Mr. Beck," he said, "but I don't see how I can help."

"He'd been to see you several times in connection with a story on which he was working," said Barrett. "Can you tell us what it was?"

"Of course. I had been thinking of producing a brochure. We get many inquiries about our facilities and the one I'm using now is rather out of date. Mr. Beck and I were cooperating on a new one. I had provided him with the details and some photographs and he was going to print it."

It sounded logical. Lou had run a little job-printing business to fill in between issues of the paper, drawing most of it from local businessmen.

"Nothing more than that?"

Horn frowned. "I fail to understand."

"Whoever killed my uncle took both the photographs and the copy for your brochure. Would you know why?"

"Fantastic," murmured Horn. "I would have no idea or even what purpose it would serve. I do have additional photos, so the thief would really accomplish nothing. As far as the copy is concerned, that is easily rewritten."

Barrett stared. "You have *duplicate* photos?"

"I always order extras for publicity uses. I do regret, however, that I also gave your uncle the negatives. He did not consider the prints I gave him suitable for reproduction purposes, and he intended to have some made that would meet his standards."

"So the thief would have been under the impression there were no other prints and there could be none since he had the negatives?"

"I imagine he would, but I still fail to see why he would bother. The photos are routine shots of the lodge, the slopes, the lifts, all our facilities. There could be absolutely nothing in them that would be of value. If anyone had asked, I would have been happy to present him a set. Furthermore, even if they had all been completely destroyed, it would present no big problem to have them retaken."

"Obviously the killer was interested only in those particular photos," said Cindy.

Barrett appealed to Horn. "May we see the duplicates?"

Horn swung around to a filing cabinet and fingered his way through a sheaf of papers until he found an envelope. He handed it to Barrett.

"I regret they are not in color," he said. "Your uncle had no facilities for that type of printing."

Barrett spread the 8 x 10 prints on Horn's desk. There were more than a dozen, taken in and around the lodge and slopes, as Horn had said, most featuring laughing people in ski clothing. Several were almost stock shots of skiers plummeting down the slopes, trailing plumes of snow.

Cindy picked up a couple of breathtaking views of the snow-covered valley, taken from the chair lift as it descended the mountain, showing the valley spread out, the roads dark slices through the snow, the lodge at the foot of the lift, the parking lot full.

"When were they taken?" she asked.

"Just last week," said Horn. "They are the most recent ones we have. I had them made especially for this brochure." He indicated the photos in her hand. "I think these are particularly well done. They show the size of the lodge so well."

The phrase *last week* jarred Barrett. Rhodes had used the same words about the girl who had been killed. "The girl who was murdered," he said to Cindy. "What day was it?"

"Last Tuesday," she said.

He looked at Horn. "And when were the photos taken?"

"The same day. It was originally scheduled for the weekend, but clouds prevented that. Luckily, we had a rather healthy crowd on Tuesday, so it was decided to do it then."

Barrett and Cindy looked at each other, each having the same thought: there might be a connection between the photos and the murder of the girl. *But what?* Barrett flipped through the photos again, seeing nothing that could possibly be relevant. "May we borrow these?" he asked Horn.

"Certainly." Horn placed the photos in an envelope and handed them to Cindy. "I will need them for my brochure eventually."

"We'll take good care of them," promised Barrett. He held the door open for Cindy, feeling that she was carrying something valuable, even though he didn't know what it was.

They were crossing the parking lot when the red VW flashed by, dangerously close, and Barrett felt a quick surge of anger. He followed the car into a parking slot just as a young man with long brown hair, dressed in a dark green ski parka, stepped out.

"Are you Pete Carey?" asked Barrett.

"Do I know you?"

"You should. You cut me off this morning and forced me off the road, then you came a little too close to us now to suit me. I don't like the way you drive."

"Drop dead," said Pete nastily.

123

It wasn't the words as much as the tone that made Barrett's hand flash out, viciously backhanding Pete across the face, driving him into the side of the VW. Barrett regretted the move the moment he made it and stepped back, ready to apologize, but Pete came off the car, a knife suddenly in his hand, his face transformed, no longer young and smooth but somehow old, ancient with hate and hurt, animalistic with a growling fury that made Barrett step back, confronted with something dark and primitive and frightening.

Barrett's breath froze in his chest and a phrase he had once read popped into his mind. *The face of madness,* he thought, and then the knife was flashing toward him and Barrett reached out, seized the arm and twisted desperately, smashing the hand against the cold steel of the car until the fingers released the knife, while Pete clawed at his face and eyes with his free hand, spitting obscenities.

Barrett pivoted, throwing Pete over his shoulder and pinning him to the ground, feeling a touch of panic because he knew that losing the knife wouldn't let Pete end it; that Pete was determined to kill him, with his bare hands if necessary; and Barrett held him there, one knee on his chest, the other on his arm, still clasping Pete's other arm with both hands, not wanting to face the thought that the fight wouldn't end until one of them was dead, when Pete suddenly became quiet and his face smoothed over and Barrett was holding an ordinary-looking young man who looked up at him with a hurt expression as if questioning what Barrett was doing.

Barrett released him and stood up. Pete lay there, staring up at him.

Barrett turned away, feeling the after-fight reaction setting in, his stomach muscles knotting and unknotting, nausea gagging him, his arms and legs trembling. He made his way to the car and collapsed into the front seat. Cindy followed, silent and almost as shaken as he was. She stared straight ahead.

Barrett breathed deeply, forcing his body to stop quivering, knowing that for the second time that day Pete Carey had pushed him to the edge of death.

"He could have killed you," whispered Cindy.

"He *would* have," said Barrett, "but it's over now and you can bet I'll stay clear of him from now on. Someday he's going to hurt someone very badly. I don't want it to be me."

"What do we do now?"

Early winter dark was setting in as Barrett

reached across the seat and took the photographs from her. "Back to the office. After Pete Carey, I need a change of pace. I'll work up the story on Lou so Cottrell can have it in the morning."

"I'll leave you there," she said. "I want to check on your aunt."

"Good," said Barrett. "Come back later and we'll go over the photos."

She dropped him off in front of the newspaper office. A headache that had been dull and quiet all day had matured into a fierce throbbing that threatened to split Barrett's head open. He crossed the street to the drugstore. It was empty now except for an elderly woman just turning away from the prescription counter and Allen Carey. Barrett decided it would be wise not to mention his fight with Carey's son.

"I need something that will work fast on a headache," he told Carey.

Carey nodded sympathetically. "Just the thing for you, Page." He poured some white pills into a small envelope and handed them to Barrett. "I find these a little better than plain aspirin. Let me get you a glass of water."

Barrett followed him to the soda fountain and gulped down two of the pills.

"Anything develop about your uncle?" asked Carey.

"Possibly." Barrett tapped the envelope. "I may have something in here that will help."

Carey craned his head to read the return address. "You picked up something at Big Bear?"

Barrett slipped the envelope under his arm. "Some publicity photos."

"Photos?" There was an odd note in Carey's voice.

"Yeah. Want to check them before turning them over to Grant Rhodes. How much do I owe you for the pills?"

Carey waved. "On the house. I hope they work for you."

Barrett had the impression he had suddenly lost Carey, that Carey's mind had fled elsewhere, that Carey never even noticed his departure.

Cottrell heard him come in and appeared in the doorway to the rear room, wiping his hand on a rag. "Nothing left for me to do. She's all locked up and ready to be put to bed, except for page one. Found an old cut of Lou I can use. All I need is the story. You going to write that?"

"Right now," Barrett told him. "It will be waiting for you in the morning."

"Make any progress?"

"We have a lead, but it's too soon to tell." He slipped out of his coat and rubbed his cold hands together. "You've had a long day, Tom. You might as well go, I'll finish the story and lock up. We'll start printing tomorrow."

"Lou would like that." Cottrell hesitated. "Just want to say, Page, that whatever you decide to do about the paper is all right with me. A man has to do what he has to do. When do you think you'll decide?"

Barrett pulled the typewriter table toward him and rolled in a sheet of copy paper. "Soon, I guess, Tom. There are many people who expect an answer."

After Cottrell left, Barrett sat staring at the keys. *Many people,* he thought; *his wife, Elmdorf, Aunt Edna, Cottrell, and even Cindy Neal, all of their small worlds temporarily orbiting around Barrett.* Wishing that the responsibility belonged to someone else, he shook his head and then began to type:

Lou G. Beck, editor and publisher of the Fox River *Tribune,* was found shot to death in his office late in the evening of..."

The words didn't come easily. It had been a long time since he had sat at a typewriter and put into practice the things that Lou had taught him. It had never been easy, he realized. Lou had just made it seem that way. He finished with a short biographical sketch of Lou and pulled the paper from the typewriter. He scanned it, made a few pencil corrections and set it aside, reaching for the photographs taken at Big Bear.

One by one, he studied them, seeing nothing that meant anything, knowing he was overlooking a detail that was important to someone else, knowing, too, that it would have had significance to his uncle; but there was no way Barrett could put himself in the old man's place, know what he knew, think his thoughts, draw the same conclusions.

No way? His uncle had a method of looking at photographs that Barrett had almost forgotten, a trick he used to be certain that some obscure background detail he didn't want couldn't slip by him.

Barrett took a blank sheet of paper and tore a hole in it about an inch square, then took the photographs in turn, placing his makeshift mask over each and sliding it across the surface, concentrating his attention only on what appeared in the ragged window. He saw things in the photographs that he hadn't noticed before, but none triggered an idea until he was sliding his mask across one of the views of the valley taken from the chair lift. As closely as he was watching, he still almost missed it, a somehow familiar bug-shaped spot against a background of snow.

He slipped the mask away and searched his uncle's desk until he found his magnifying glass and focused it on the spot.

There was no question now. Enlarged, it was a VW with skis strapped to its rear deck. Seeing one at this time of the year in the valley was ordinary enough. There were many, including Pete Carey's. What intrigued Barrett was that this one didn't seem to be traveling along any of the snow-covered back roads. Instead, it was some distance from the nearest one, evidently following a service track through the snow that some farmer used to reach the back sections of his property in winter. The thought struck Barrett that the car was parked, but why in such an out-of-the-way spot? If there were an answer, he didn't know what it was.

Barrett tossed the picture aside and picked up another to find he could no longer concentrate on what he was doing. That VW in the middle of nowhere bothered him. Maybe Cindy would have an explanation for it when she came back. He closed his eyes and leaned back in the chair, thinking that he was more tired than he realized. Carey's pills had eliminated the headache but they also must have contained some sort of sedative. Barrett felt a warm lassitude creeping upward from his legs.

He hadn't heard the door open, but a cold draft made him look up as Allen Carey came through the swinging gate.

"Pete told me what happened," said Carey.

"I apologize for that. I was sorry I lost my temper."

Carey waved away his apology. "Pete gave you a lot of trouble, didn't he?"

"You could say that. In my opinion, he needs some sort of psychiatric attention before he hurts someone."

"I don't think it's that bad. He's just a confused young boy. He'll grow out of it."

He was no longer a boy and there was no chance he would grow out of it, Barrett knew, but then it wasn't his concern. He had problems of his own. He merely nodded, saying nothing.

Carey had been edging forward into the office. Barrett realized he was staring at the photos on the desk.

"May I see those?" There was a strange note in Carey's voice.

"I think not. They are the only set and I'm responsible for them."

"Lou had photos of Big Bear yesterday. I suppose these are different?"

Barrett was no longer tired. As far as he knew, only Cindy, Horn, and himself were aware that the killer had taken the original set. "No," he said cautiously. "These are the same. Horn had duplicates."

Carey's face was the color of Camembert that had aged too long. "You looked at them?"

"Of course," said Barrett.

"Ah," said Carey, sounding as if he were gagging. "Let me see the pictures."

"What for?"

Carey's hand went under his coat and came out with a gun, the kind that almost every kid in the county used for small game and target practice. Barrett froze. Carey's hand might be trembling, but at this range he wasn't shaking enough to miss.

"I didn't want this to happen. I never thought it would happen." Carey sounded as if he might start weeping at any moment. Perspiration glistened on his forehead. His eyes flicked around the room as if driven by tumbling thoughts.

"You'll have to tell me," Barrett said. "Give me a reason for the gun."

"Lou brought a picture to me yesterday.

There was something he wanted to ask about."

Barrett, his mind half-numbed by the gun, was trying to sort it all out when it became clear; beautifully clear. "A Volkswagen," he said. "Parked where it had no right to be. Near where the girl was killed. Lou wanted to know if it was Pete's car, where Pete had been that day."

Carey nodded. "I see you think the same as Lou. He said he was going to have Grant Rhodes ask Pete about it. I couldn't allow that."

"Because you knew that Pete had killed the girl. Once Grant Rhodes started to question him –"

"No," Carey interrupted. "Pete didn't kill the girl."

Barrett thought of the secret Pete Carey he had glimpsed that afternoon. Someone like that could have easily raped and strangled.

"Yes," he said. "Pete killed her. So you came in here last night, killed Lou, one of your best friends, and took the photos and the negatives to protect a son you know should be locked up somewhere."

"That wasn't the way it was," cried Carey. "That's not how it was at all. There is nothing wrong with Pete. Nothing, you hear

133

me? All Pete could have told Rhodes was that he didn't have the car that afternoon, that someone had borrowed it."

"Then you're a fool, Allen. Who borrowed the car?"

"Don't you understand?" Carey's voice was almost a wail. "It was *me!*"

The only sound in the room was Carey's labored breathing. *Ah, now,* thought Barrett, *not Carey himself. Not Carey, the pharmacist who had helped so many people, responsible now for two killings and intent on a third.*

"Why, Allen?" he asked gently. "I can see that you felt you had to kill Lou to get the pictures, but why the girl in the first place?"

"You just don't know what it's like in this town, seeing your life slip away. The years go and suddenly you're old and you haven't done anything."

"What does that have to do with it?"

Carey passed a hand over his face. "She made me feel young again. For just a minute... Then it happened. She was going to tell." He straightened suddenly, eyes no longer shifting, no longer trembling. "It doesn't matter now." The gun leveled at Barrett's head. "I have do do this, Page. I can't let anyone find out. You shouldn't have interfered. You don't belong here any more."

Barrett realized that talking would do no

good. There was a set to Carey's expression and a light in his eyes that reminded Barrett of Pete Carey holding a knife. Carey was far beyond listening. He would hear only what he wanted to hear.

Barrett picked up the photograph and held it out. "This is what you want, Allen. Why not take it and go?"

"No. There would be nothing to keep you from telling Grant Rhodes."

Barrett casually placed his feet on the cross-brace of the heavy typewriter table. He tossed the photo at Carey and as Carey's eyes followed it, he violently pushed the typewriter stand toward him, using both feet and hands. If Carey had been a professional, he would have killed Barrett before the photo fluttered to the floor, but Carey was an overwrought, confused pharmacist. The typewriter stand, heavy machine tottering, catapulted across the office and smashed Carey across the thighs, doubling him up, the pistol falling as Carey dropped his hands to protect himself.

Barrett dived across the office and scooped up the pistol. Carey, bent over the stand, looked at him pleadingly, lips moving in some sort of silent entreaty. Barrett almost felt sorry for the crazed druggist.

They were standing like that when Rhodes

and Cindy Neal came through the door. Rhodes looked at the pistol in Barrett's hands. "What's that thing for? Allen charge you too much for a prescription?"

Barrett handed it to him. "Save the jokes. I think you'll find this killed Lou." He indicated Carey. "He pulled the trigger. He'll tell you why, but if he doesn't, you'll still develop enough to hold him on two counts of murder."

"Two counts?"

"He also killed the girl last week."

Rhodes had been a police officer too long to let any emotion show, but Barrett knew the news must have jolted him clear down to his polished shoes.

"I thought I was coming here to look at some photos," Rhodes said slowly. "Cindy called me and said you might have something. I didn't expect this. Suppose you start at the beginning."

Barrett explained while Carey stood there, a small, putty-faced fat man who didn't look dangerous at all, and Cindy leaned on the counter, eyes fixed on Barrett.

"That's the third time today you almost got yourself killed," said Cindy wonderingly when he had finished.

"I seem to have that trouble with the Carey family," said Barrett dryly. "But he showed the gun too soon. Lou turned his back on him before he knew Carey had one. We should have guessed that Lou knew the man who killed him, knew him well enough to let him get behind him without suspecting anything."

Rhodes placed a hand on Carey's arm. "I'll take him over to the station. You stop by later and we'll talk some more." He led Carey out.

Cindy sighed. "At least it is all over now."

"Almost," said Barrett. "There is still the paper to print and Lou's funeral to be attended."

"And then?" There was an unsaid hope in her voice, a hope that the paper wouldn't die as Lou had died, a hope that Barrett would stay.

She looked young, exceedingly beautiful, and very vulnerable. It was a look that Barrett hadn't seen on a woman's face in a long time.

Instead of being tempted, he merely felt old.

Allen Carey had been right on two counts when he said, "You don't belong here, Page."

The first was that Barrett was a different breed from a different age, from a faster moving, entirely different world, and he was

137

no Lou Beck, with little of the old man's talent and skill. Barrett couldn't run the paper, not the way the old man had run it.

The second was that Barrett's problem wasn't with his wife but with himself. He had clung too long to the dream that many men had; that it was possible to go back, to erase the years that brought him to this time and place. He had carved out an existence that might not be all he hoped it would be, but in many ways it was satisfying and, above all, it belonged to him and was no poor imitation of someone else.

Carey's words echoed: "You don't belong here, Page."

Barrett sighed. When they buried Lou Beck, they would bury part of Page Barrett, too: the part that had grown up here and developed here, though that part had been dead a long time, much longer than Lou Beck. Barrett had simply never realized it.

He looked at Cindy, smiled, and said, "And then I'll go home."

Hit or Miss

by Edward Wellen

Finley Crowe stepped into the Hotel Granville, cased the lobby, went to the phone booth at the far end, and riffled his right hand through the pages of the Manhattan directory as his left hand reached below to remove a slip of paper taped to the underside of the shelf.

Still pretending to be hunting a number and using his body as a shield, he brought up the paper, unfolded it, and read it. All it said was *819*. Finley Crowe now knew that the man he had to kill was staying in Room 819 of the Hotel Granville.

He balled the slip of paper and tossed it at the first sand urn he passed. Too sure of his aim, he failed to see that he had missed the desert waste. The ball hit the rim and bounded to the carpet.

Carefully watching carelessly to make sure that no one noticed him, Finley Crowe gained the stairs and started up.

Leroy Moore bent to pick up the ball of paper. He straightened slowly, silently cursing his aching back. He started to drop the crumple of paper into the sand urn, then something moved him to stay his hand.

He unwadded the paper and smoothed it out enough to read it. All it said was *618*. Leroy Moore made up his mind to hurry and play 618 and play it big. It would have been a sin to overlook this sign.

Clifford Fant, in Room 618, had a hangup hangup. His hand shook so that it took three stabs before he hung up the phone.

The girl had disguised her voice, but he knew who it had to be. Making time with her, though she was hardly his type, was paying off now. It wasn't luck but fore-thought that had given him a pair of ears in syndicate headquarters – and now a voice.

"There's a contract out on you. You'd better hurry out of there. The hit man knows where you are."

Then, before he could ask questions or even frame questions to ask, *click!*

It was new to him to be on the same side of the law – the wrong side – as his clients. He had always managed to stay on the right side while advancing the fortunes of those on the wrong side. A syndicate mouthpiece,

140

he had lately begun practicing the art of avoiding subpoenas.

Now it seemed that his former clients were taking no chances on the privileged communications between client and lawyer remaining privileged. They were not trusting to the canon of ethics alone to seal his lips, and since syndicate headquarters itself had put out the contract, it meant there was no appeal.

He tried to pull himself together, but the walls of the room closed in like a trap. *You'd better hurry out of there. The hit man knows where you are.* He didn't dare check out. He would just disappear. He would carry what effects he could on his person and sneak out. He looked around.

His gun, of course; he had started packing a gun these past few weeks, sensing that something like this might happen. It was one more thing putting him on the wrong side of the law because in his fugitive state he could hardly have openly sought a permit. Even as he stuck the gun in his waistband he knew it would avail little against the skilled hit man they would have sent after him. Still, its solid weight was some comfort.

Now to fill his pockets with razor, toothbrush, socks, shorts; really not much else worth taking or risking taking. *You'd better hurry out of there*. Quick. Otherwise, dead.

Murray Lenox, in Room 819, shot too much lather out of the can of shaving foam. His finger had been too heavy on the valve because he had been thinking savage thoughts about Ms. Missy.

Ms. Missy; he had invented the name so that she might ride the wave of women's lib. He had plucked her out of a nothing rock group going nowhere. Did she guess why he had picked her? Her voice and delivery were nothing special. Did she knew he loved her?

He had spent months on the road, hitting every radio station with a disc jockey having a halfway decent following. It took a lot of buttering – and a lot of bread – but he had publicized and payola'd her recording into a hit number. Now that she was high on the charts and had hit the Big Apple, Ms. Missy had a swelled head.

She had come right out and said that maybe Murray's cut of the take was too much, that maybe for the same amount she could get a big-time agent-manager who would make her more than a one-shot.

He had just looked at her, turned, and walked away. Walked away with stiff dignity, though expecting her to call after him and say she was sorry and beg him to come back.

She hadn't called after him, and she hadn't rung up yet, but give her time. She would miss him, realize how much she owed him and how much she still needed him.

He slapped the foam on his face. He had enough to build a Santa Claus beard. He looked in the mirror, he looked in his heart. Some Santa Claus. He reached for his razor, stopped at a knocking.

Missy!

He limped eagerly to the door.

Finley Crowe rapped again on the door of Room 819. He had waited a few minutes on the landing before venturing into the eighth-floor corridor. That was as much to get his breath back after the climb as to screw the silencer onto his gun.

The years of being a hit man were telling on him. No, it was just the years. The hit stuff didn't bother him.

The door of Room 819 opened.

Crowe stared, but it was only the lather that had taken him aback. The right build, the right color hair, and the right color eyes; this was Clifford Fant, all right.

He and Cliff went back to the old days, but

143

he had never let sentiment get in the way of his work.

The man's head jerked at the sight of the gun. His hands went up to push the sight away.

The man had time to say, "No."

Yes.

Just as Clifford Fant eased past the last doorway on the sixth floor and silently made it onto the stairs, he came face to face with Finley Crowe coming as silently down.

In Crowe, the feeling that he was seeing a ghost prompted the motor reflex of his gun hand. If it was the knowledge that he had already done his number that slowed Crowe, it was the knowledge that his hit man had found him that sped Fant.

It was a draw. They held each other at gunpoint.

Fant said, without hope, "Let's talk this over."

Crowe's reply was a real shocker. "Sure."

Crowe's credit card let them into Room 819.

They looked down at the stiff just inside the door. Fant shivered. But for the 618-819 mixup, which he and Crowe had figured out together, that shattered, spattered face would be his. He shivered again. He could still wind up a corpse if Crowe should decide they couldn't pull it off. He edged away and inched his hand toward the gun in his waistband.

Crowe, turning to face him, smiled at what he plainly took to be Fant's squeamishness. "You registered here under another name, didn't you?"

Fant nodded.

Crowe nodded. "So it don't matter if the cops never find out who the stiff is, as long as the mob thinks it's you. Only problem might be the stiff's fingerprints. If I thought I had to, I'd scrape the guy's fingers raw. But look at his feet."

Fant frowned puzzledly. "Are you talking about *toe*prints?"

Crowe permitted himself a flash of irritation. "No. I mean, look at his shoes. One shoe's built up a bit. Means he was never in the armed services. That, together with the odds he's a square john, means his fingerprints won't be on file. I'll just check his I.D., make sure." He went through the stiff's pockets. "The guy's legit – if being a talent representative's legit. Now, change shoes with him." He handed Fant the stiff's wallet and keys.

Fant stared at Crowe. "What?"

"Change shoes with him. That'll be good

enough; who's going to notice the inch difference when they lay him out?"

Fant grimaced as he walked back and forth in the dead man's shoes. The stiff's shoes fitted Fant fine, but they gave him a limp. Still, that would prove a plus worth getting used to when he went forth in his new incarnation.

Crowe got up from tying the shoestrings on Fant's shoes on Lenox's feet in neat bows.

"Okay, Fant. Now we're all set for the switch."

Fant stole out into the corridor, found a linen cart in the service closet, and sneaked it back to Room 819. He and Crowe wrapped Lenox in a sheet. When Fant bent to pick up his end of Lenox, his gun fell out of his waistband. Crowe picked it up and politely handed it to Fant. They stuffed Lenox into the linen cart, rolled the cart to the service elevator, and took it down to the sixth floor. Fant found he had kept his key; he let the three of them into Room 618.

Fant and Crowe lifted Lenox out of the cart, unwrapped him, and arranged him on the floor.

Crowe fitted the silencer onto his gun again. For a moment Fant felt faint, but Crowe simply drove another bullet through the body to pin the killing to this room.

Crowe unscrewed the silencer and pocketed it and the gun. Then he fiddled with the air conditioner till it stopped working. This gave him the excuse to open the window. The open window took care of the missing first bullet.

Together, Crowe and Fant went over 618, wiping all surfaces that might have taken fingerprints.

Before leaving Room 618 for the last time, Clifford Fant looked down at the body of Murray Lenox, and felt a sudden sympathy for Clifford Fant.

Fant and Crowe went out with the linen cart and hung the DO NOT DISTURB sign outside the door of Room 618.

They got the linen cart safely back in its eighth-floor closet and Fant let them into Room 819 with Lenox's key. Crowe helped Fant clean up the mess in the room. Crowe found the bullet embedded in the wall. He gouged it out and pocketed it, then looked around and sighed. Fant echoed the sigh. There seemed nothing more to do but part.

This working out of their mutual bind suited both; Fant, because it meant he stayed alive but passed for dead – which would help him stay alive under a new name and in a new place; Crowe, because it meant he kept his name for always making a clean hit.

Before leaving, Crowe rested his eyes on Fant's face, the look saying that his eyes had better not ever rest on Fant's face again.

Fant took no chances on Crowe's changing his mind. He quickly packed Lenox's bags, then phoned the desk to say he – Murray Lenox – was checking out. He worried as he signed the tab with Lenox's name, but none of the Hotel Granville's personnel – desk clerk, bellhop, or doorman – focused on anything but the formalities and the gratuities.

He changed cabs several times, winding up at the Port Authority Bus Terminal. His gun would force him to forego planes and to go by bus, train, and rented car, but that made it all the easier to lose himself. He would travel on Lenox's credit cards till it became dangerous to do so; the monthly billing date would be the deadline. Then Murray Lenox would disappear, say while out boating or swimming in very deep waters.

At which point Clifford Fant would take on a new identity and live out his borrowed life above one border or below the other as best he might.

Ms. Missy used the Hotel Granville's courtesy phone to call Room 819. Room 819 did not answer. Ms. Missy's rocker platforms carried her to the desk clerk. She was not too worried to give him her best smile. Mr. Lenox? Sorry, Mr. Lenox had just checked out; she had missed him by minutes. Sorry, Mr. Lenox left no forwarding address. Ms. Missy's smile died.

It was Leroy Moore's lucky day. Number 618 hit.

He told his boss that he was quitting, and there were hard feelings when he told the man what he thought of him.

Leroy Moore made big plans to spend his big money, but when it came time for him to collect his winnings, he found that the runner with whom he had placed the bet had kept his twenty dollars instead of passing it on to the policy bank. The runner had figured 618 would not come out. It had, and the runner had decided his best bet was to be among the missing.

The syndicate boss's words came out wrapped in cigar smoke.

"We only got this Leroy Moore's word he played twenty bucks on 618. Be good public relations, though, to give him his twenty bucks back. If that don't suit him, maybe he'd like a few broken bones better. Now, about the runner that took off: quick as we find him we finish him. Get Finley Crowe to do the job. There's a guy that don't never mess up a hit."

Murder in Miniature

By Nora Caplan

Ann waited eagerly for her husband's response, but he said nothing for a long while. He remained standing, his face speculative as he looked down at the large dollhouse in the basement closet. It was pure Victorian ... a three storied wooden structure painted dark green with a mansard roof centered by a cupola and white gingerbread scrollwork ornamenting the front porch. Finally, he commented, "I thought you said Holly wanted a microscope for her birthday."

"Oh, Phil." Both annoyance and amusement were in her voice. "A microscope for an eight-year-old girl? *This* is what she needs. Have you ever seen anything like it?" Ann's delight was obvious as she pointed out the rooms, furnished to the last detail in authentic period pieces. "And when I saw the dolls ... look, there's even a maid." She sighed, "Well, I couldn't resist it."

Phil shrugged. "Maybe she'll like it. You

151

know more about that than I do. I just don't want her to be disappointed, that's all. She's never cared much about dolls before, has she?"

"This is different," his wife said defensively. "Besides, Holly needs something unusual like this to stimulate her imagination. That's the whole trouble, Phil. She's never been given a chance to pretend anything. We've just always gone along with that matter-of-fact side of her."

"But that *is* Holly." As if to end the discussion, Phil walked over to the hot water heater. "This thing's leaking again. You'd better give the company a call before long. The warranty's up in a couple of months."

Ann was determined to justify her reason for buying the dollhouse, so disregarding his last remarks, she said, "I've never been able to share anything much with Holly. She's not the way I was at her age or like any other child I grew up with. She's never known the fun of pretending the way we did, and she's growing up so fast." Ann bent over the dollhouse and very gently fingered a miniature steamer trunk in the attic. "I've been looking for something the two of us could enjoy together. I knew this was it the minute I saw it."

Phil returned to her, and patted her on the

shoulder. "Okay, if you think it'll make her happy. Come on upstairs now, honey. It's cold down here."

With his saying it, she shivered. Suddenly she felt depressed. Tomorrow was Holly's birthday. It was too late to get her anything else. She wondered if Phil could be right in doubting that Holly would like the dollhouse. No, Ann concluded shortly. It must appeal to her. It simply wasn't possible for a daughter of hers to be totally lacking a sense of imagination.

The next morning after Holly left for school, Phil and Ann moved the dollhouse upstairs to their daughter's room. "Should I try to keep her downstairs until you get home?" Ann asked her husband.

"The suspense would kill you," Phil grinned. He kissed the tip of her nose. "Don't wait for me. Go ahead and show it to her the minute she gets home."

Holly looked exactly like Phil, Ann thought that afternoon as she watched her daughter scrutinize the dollhouse for the first time. She had the same even expression in her deep-set brown eyes, the identical composed shape of her mouth. And as her mother had expected, Holly made a thorough inspection of each room before she stated an opinion. "This is different from Sara's. It's supposed to be in the olden days, isn't it?"

Ann smiled and stooped beside her. "The style is called Victorian. It's about eighty or ninety years old. Things were very different then. Look at the kitchen pump. It really works, too." She showed Holly how the handle moved up and down.

"I see," Holly nodded.

Ann couldn't wait any longer. "Do you like it, darling? Isn't it lots better than a microscope?"

Holly noted the elation in her mother's vivid blue eyes. "Well," she answered carefully, "it'll give me lots to learn about."

Some hours later when Ann went into Holly's room to see if she was reading in semi-darkness as usual, she found Holly lying on her side, staring at the dollhouse. The small tole lamp shining opposite it almost spotlighted the rooms, so that they gave the impression of stage settings for an Ibsen play. Ann reached to turn off the light.

"Please leave it on," Holly said without turning her head.

Ann smiled, and answered lightly but with purpose, "You know, you're keeping the Joneses from retiring."

Holly looked up at her mother. A puzzled frown wrinkled her forehead at first, then it

154

disappeared. "Oh, you mean *them*." She faced the dollhouse again. "Their name is Pettingill." She yawned. "The Bartholomew J. Pettingills. And the maid's name is Clara Fisher."

Though the following day was Saturday, Phil went to his office at the Bureau of Standards. Before he left, he murmured something about having to get the notes for his next lecture, but Ann was too preoccupied to pay much attention. Holly had already finished breakfast, and had gone back up to her room. On a pretext of starting the upstairs cleaning, Ann took a dust cloth to Holly's bedroom. Her daughter was sitting quietly in a rocker before the dollhouse. "Do you suppose," she asked her mother, "you could make them some new clothes?"

"I'd love to." Ann bent down and started to pick up Mrs. Pettingill.

"Don't, Mommy!" Holly's voice was sharp. "She hates to be touched."

Ann hastily withdrew her hand. "Oh, really?" The tiny figure's china face was rather proud and stern. Then Ann studied the father. "Mr. Pettingill seems pleasant enough."

"He is." Holly removed him from a Lincoln rocker in the parlor. She rubbed her

155

finger over his black painted mustache. "That's the trouble."

"What do you mean...trouble?" Ann sat down on the floor, completely enthralled.

"Well, you see," Holly explained very seriously, "she thinks he's not strict enough with Charlie, for one thing."

"Their little boy?" Ann pointed to the doll in a sailor suit astride a hobby horse in the second floor nursery.

"Mm-hmm," Holly nodded. "He's really a nice little boy, but he does things that make his mother mad."

"For instance?"

"Oh, just little things. Getting his shoes muddy and forgetting to put his things away."

Ann's eyes twinkled. "What's so wrong with that? As a matter of fact, she doesn't sound very different from me, or any other mother."

Holly continued in the same earnest manner, "But she won't let him alone. She always wants him to do what she thinks is best for him and not what he'd really like to do at all. And another thing, she can't stand a bit of dust anywhere. She really works poor Clara...the maid...terribly hard. I think Clara would've left a long time ago if it hadn't been for Mr. Pettingill and Charlie."

She stroked Clara's blonde pompadour. "I want you to make Clara a beautiful dress with a parasol to match."

Ann's mouth turned up. "But, darling, she's the maid."

Holly said stubbornly, "I don't care. Besides, she doesn't have to work on Sundays, and she always takes Charlie for a walk in the park after church. Sometimes Mr. Pettingill goes along with them, too. So she needs a pretty dress."

"And what about the new clothes for Mrs. Pettingill?"

Holly was indifferent. "Oh, you don't have to bother with her. What she has on is all right."

Ann felt curiously defensive about the mother doll. She couldn't understand Holly's hostile attitude toward Mrs. Pettingill. More to herself than to her daughter, Ann replied, "The mother's dress could be dark blue...taffeta, I think. With a white lace collar."

"I think I'll read for a while." Holly rose and went over to the bookcase under the dormer window.

Ann knew that she was being dismissed. She got to her feet and started to leave when Holly added, "I'd like Clara's dress to be pink with a real full skirt and ruffles around the bottom. Charlie and Mr. Pettingill would like that, too."

As Ann changed the linens on the bed in Phil's and her room, she kept thinking about her conversation with Holly. She was pleased, naturally, that her daughter's imagination had apparently begun to emerge. And yet, it had taken such a strange turn. There was something so...real about the Pettingills. They weren't at all like the improbably good, pretend families she remembered from her own childhood. Still, they were far more intriguing, and evidently real to Holly.

She went over to a chest and pulled out the bottom drawer. She rummaged through it and finally came up with a scrap of Alençon lace. There was more than enough of it for a collar, but the taffeta...She found a piece of dark blue satin. That would do even better. Mrs. Pettingill would be a model of good taste compared with the frilled pink organdy flounces of Clara, with matching parasol.

The following Monday afternoon Ann was in the kitchen making seven-minute frosting when she heard Holly come home from school. Her daughter called from the living room, "Mommy, Sara's here. Her mother said she could stay till five o'clock."

Ann raised her voice over the clatter of the beater. "Hang up your things in the hall closet." She expected the girls to come into the kitchen, but shortly she heard them run upstairs. Abruptly she turned off the mixer. Sara was such a helter-skelter sort of child, there was no telling what she might do to the dollhouse. And there were the new clothes on the Pettingills and Clara. She'd planned to surprise Holly with them, but it wouldn't be the same now with Sara around. Her face hardened. She would go upstairs anyway.

The two girls didn't notice her when she came to the doorway. "It's sort of funny looking," Sara was saying. "I like my dollhouse better. Mine's got electric lights, too." She seized Mrs. Pettingill by one arm, crushing the leg o'mutton sleeve that Ann had struggled over.

"Put her down," Ann commanded. The girls stared. Ann removed the doll from Sara's sticky fingers, and as she tried to fluff the sleeve into fullness again, she said coldly, "You'd better play down in the recreation room."

"But, Mommy," Holly protested.

"Go ahead. Do as I say." They left, subdued and silent, but she stayed by the dollhouse for a time. Finally she returned to the kitchen. Thanks to Sara, the frosting was ruined. She dumped it into the sink, and turned on the water with such force that it soaked her apron.

Holly was so constrained at dinner that night that Phil asked her, "What's the matter? Something happen at school today?"

"No." She avoided looking at her mother and addressed Phil, "Can I be excused now?"

He glanced at her plate. She'd hardly touched her food.

"It's all right." Ann made the decision for him. As soon as Holly slipped from the dining room, Ann explained, "Sara was over this afternoon. She always overstimulates Holly."

"I've never noticed it before," he said.

"Well, she does." Ann pushed back her chair, and began stacking the plates.

"You think Holly might be coming down with something? She's seemed pretty quiet the last couple of days."

"I don't think so. She's just tired, that's all."

After she'd finished the dishes, Ann carried a cup of coffee into the living room. Phil was watching a news report on TV. She drank the coffee thoughtfully. Maybe she had been a little too sharp with Holly this afternoon, but Sara had grated on her nerves so. She didn't see what there was about that child that attracted Holly to her. Then Ann remembered that she hadn't had a chance to discuss the new doll clothes with Holly. By now she'd probably got over her moodiness.

She found Holly stretched out on her bed, face down. Ann smoothed the child's hair. "You're not asleep, are you, baby?"

"No."

Ann sat down beside her. "I forgot to ask you what you think of the Pettingills' and Clara's new outfits."

"They're okay," Holly replied in a monotone.

"I had a terrible time with Mrs. Pettingill's dress. The sleeves still don't fit quite right below the elbows, but it's so hard to work on anything that small." Ann questioned gently, "Do you suppose she'll mind?" Holly didn't answer. Ann supposed that she was still resentful about not being allowed to play in her room. "I've been thinking that maybe we should fix up Mr. and Mrs. Pettingill's room. It's so drab compared with the rest of the house. I have some lovely pale green silk that I could make into draperies and a bedspread, and ..."

"I don't want you to," Holly interrupted shrilly, and sat up on the edge of the bed. Her shoulders were rigid.

"But why not, sweetie?" There was a soft insistence in Ann's voice.

Holly repeated uneasily, "I don't want you..." She swallowed. "I mean, I don't think Mrs. Pettingill would like that."

"Of course she would," Ann argued more firmly. "Pastel green was just the sort of color that was fashionable in those days, and it would do a lot more for that dark walnut bed and highboy than that dingy lace."

Holly picked at one of the yarn ties on her comforter. "But it would make Clara feel bad."

"What's she got to do with it? She's only the maid." Ann glanced with annoyance at the uniformed figure in the kitchen. Clara's blue eyes stared back at her. At that moment there seemed to be something challenging about her vapid smile.

Holly misinterpreted her mother's silence as interest. "Clara's so much nicer than Mrs. Pettingill. She understands Charlie and Mr. Pettingill. I think they really like her better."

Ann was rather shocked. "But, Holly, that's not natural."

"I want to go to bed now." Holly untied one shoe slowly, then placed it on the floor beside her bed.

"All right, chicken." Ann kissed her daughter's cheek.

162

Holly kept her eyes on the floor. "Don't do anything more to the dollhouse. Please, Mother."

"We'll talk about it later, dear. You're tired now. Go to sleep."

For the next week the Pettingills weren't mentioned. Holly played at Sara's house every afternoon until dinnertime. After-wards, she did her homework, read, or watched TV until bedtime. Phil was having Ann type a draft of his lecture, and she didn't have time to talk much to her daughter. She grew increasingly keyed-up, with Phil's demands that the copy be absolutely accurate, in spite of her having to decipher his illegible handwriting. And all the time she was bothered by Holly's strange reaction that last particular night.

She finished Phil's report Friday morning. At lunch she said to Holly, "I'm all through with Daddy's work now. Let's do something special this afternoon."

Holly captured a bit of carrot from her spoonful of vegetable soup, and put it aside on a plate. "I promised Sara I'd go over to her house. She told me she has a surprise for me."

Ann felt that she had to make a compromise in order not to estrange her daughter further. With resignation she said. "Well, bring Sara here then." When Holly hesitated, Ann added. "You've been at her place so much lately, I'm sure her mother needs a rest by now."

"Okay," Holly agreed. She glanced at the clock over the refrigerator. "I'd better go now. Sara said she'd meet me at the corner at twelve thirty."

Ann resolved to be as pleasant as possible to Sara that afternoon. She baked some brownies, and made a pitcher of lemonade. She set the kitchen table for a tea party. Holly would like this. Ann went upstairs to the spare bedroom, took from the closet a box of clothes to be mended, and sat down at the sewing machine.

"Mommy," Holly called from the foyer an hour or so later, "we're here. Come and see what Sara gave me."

Ann smiled at the two of them as she came down the stairs. Holly held out her hand. In it was a tiny circlet of white fur.

Sara's freckled face was exuberant. "It's a muff for Clara. I made it all by myself." She stopped abruptly as she saw the change of expression in Ann's eyes. She looked down. "Well, my mother did help a little. She showed me . . ."

164

"Why did you do it?" Ann's smile was fixed.

"Well, I . . ." Sara stammered.

"She wanted to, Mommy," Holly spoke up. "What's wrong?"

Ann was gripping the newel post so hard that her knuckles had turned white. "But why *Clara?*" The two girls registered nothing but bewilderment, and soon Ann said tonelessly, "There's a snack for you in the kitchen. I have to finish the mending."

But when she returned to the spare bedroom, she replaced the box of clothes in the closet. She went to her own room to get the remnant of pale green silk.

Ann timed the surprise perfectly. While Holly was taking her bath that night, Ann tiptoed into her room and knelt beside the dollhouse. What a difference the new curtains and bedspread made in Mrs. Pettingill's room. And the moss green velvet pillow on the slipper chair was an inspiration. As her final touch, Ann slipped a minute string of pearls around Mrs. Pettingill's throat.

"What're you doing?" Holly had entered with a towel draped around her shoulders, and water was still trickling down her legs.

Ann stood up. "Oh, I just made a little

165

surprise for the dollhouse." She saw her daughter was trembling. "Dry yourself off first, dear. You can see it after you've put on your pajamas."

Holly remained near the door, shivering. "But I didn't want you to, Mommy," she said tearfully. "I told you not to do anything more to the dollhouse."

"You'll catch cold like that. Here, let me help you." Ann began rubbing Holly down briskly with the towel. "Now put on your pajamas quick." Holly was so slow about it that Ann finished buttoning the top herself. "There, now," her mother said. "Let's go see the surprise."

"No," Holly shuddered. "I'm still cold. I just want to go to bed and get warm."

Ann's disappointment changed to concern. "Do you feel sick, darling?"

Holly hunched herself under the covers. "My stomach feels funny."

"It's from all those brownies and lemonade this afternoon. I know Sara makes a habit of stuffing herself, but you should know better." Ann frowned. "Maybe some milk of magnesia . . ."

"I'll be all right."

"You're sure."

Holly nodded.

Ann kissed her. "Call me if you should

start to feel sick." She turned to look at Holly once more before she went downstairs. The child lay absolutely still, her eyes fixed on the dollhouse.

The cry in the middle of the night was unrecognizable at first, but Phil and Ann awoke to full consciousness. Then from Holly's room came a terrified, "Daddy... Daddy."

Ann flung back the sheet and blanket. "Stay here," she said tersely to her husband. "I'll go to her."

Holly was huddled against her pillow. She wouldn't look up when Ann bent over her, murmuring, "What's wrong, baby?"

"Take it away," Holly gasped.

"Take what away?"

"The dollhouse. Take it away...now," Holly pleaded.

"In the middle of the night? But why, darling? Did you have a bad dream?"

"Just take it away...please. Right now." Holly's voice rose, shrill to the verge of hysteria.

Phil appeared in the doorway. He'd apparently heard what she'd said, for he commented smoothly, reasonably, "But we can't move it out at this hour, honey. All the stuff inside has to be taken out so nothing

167

will get broken. We'll take care of it the first thing in the morning."

But Holly was unassuaged. She kept crying, "No . . . take it away . . . now."

"Tell you what," Phil said after a moment's deliberation. "Suppose we put something over the dollhouse so you can't see it." He motioned to Ann to get the extra blanket at the foot of Holly's bed.

"What do you suppose frightened her so?" Ann whispered to Phil as he stepped over to her.

"Never mind that now," he muttered. "The poor kid's upset enough already." Then he raised his voice to the same unruffled tone as before. "Holly, remember that time when you were about four or five, and you kept seeing those shadows from your tree swing on this wall . . ."

Ann unfolded the blanket. She was about to drape it over the dollhouse. But she sensed that something was terribly wrong. *Mrs. Pettingill. Where was she?* Ann searched every room in the dollhouse with mounting tension. Clara and Charlie and Mr. Pettingill were seated in the parlor, their china faces placid and content. The scene was entirely too innocent.

Ann found the clue she was looking for.

168

The pearl necklace. *Clara was wearing Mrs. Pettingill's pearl necklace.*

Almost instinctively now, Ann knew where she would find Mrs. Pettingill. She reached up to the storage room in the attic. Her fingers felt numb as she unlocked and opened the steamer trunk. Mrs. Pettingill was inside . . . *crushed* . . . her neck broken.

Ann slowly turned around. With the trunk between her thumb and forefinger, she held it up for Holly to see. "Why did you let them do it?"

Holly leaned toward her father. "It . . . it was an accident." She pressed closer to Phil. "I didn't mean to. Honest."

Phil tightened his arm around the child. "For God's sake, Ann," he began angrily. Then he stopped. He'd never before seen the kind of emotion that was now darkening his wife's eyes.

Deadly calm, Ann said, "No, Holly. It wasn't an accident." She replaced the trunk in the attic, with poor Mrs. Pettingill still inside. "It was no accident," she confronted Clara and Mr. Pettingill. "*You* murdered her."

Smuggler's Island

by Bill Pronzini

The first I heard that somebody had bought Smuggler's Island was late on a cold foggy morning in May. Handy Manners and Davey and I had just brought the *Jennie Too* into the Camaroon Bay wharf, loaded with the day's limit in salmon – silvers mostly, with a few big kings – and Handy had gone inside the processing shed at Bay Fisheries to call for the tally clerk and the portable scales. I was helping Davey hoist up the hatch covers, and I was thinking that he handled himself fine on the boat and what a shame it'd be if he decided eventually that he didn't want to go into commercial fishing as his livelihood. A man likes to see his only son take up his chosen profession. But Davey was always talking about traveling around Europe, seeing some of the world, maybe finding a career he liked better than fishing. Well, he was only nineteen. Decisions don't come quick or easy at that age.

170

Anyhow, we were working on the hatch covers when I heard somebody call my name. I glanced up, and Pa and Abner Frawley were coming toward us from down-wharf, where the cafe was. I was a little surprised to see Pa out on a day like this; he usually stayed home with Jennie when it was overcast and windy because the fog and cold air aggravated his lumbago.

The two of them came up and stopped, Pa puffing on one of his home-carved meerschaum pipes. They were both seventy-two and long-retired – Abner from a manager's job at the cannery a mile up the coast, Pa from running the general store in the village – and they'd been cronies for at least half their lives. But that was where all resemblance between them ended. Abner was short and round and white-haired, and always had a smile and a joke for everybody. Pa, on the other hand, was tall and thin and dour; if he'd smiled any more than four times in the forty-seven years since I was born I can't remember it. Abner had come up from San Francisco during the Depression, but Pa was a second-generation native of Camaroon Bay, his father having emigrated from Ireland during the short-lived potato boom in the early 1900's. He was a good man and a decent father, which was why I'd given

171

him a room in our house when Ma died six years ago, but I'd never felt close to him.

He said to me, "Looks like a good catch, Verne."

"Pretty good," I said. "How come you're out in this weather?"

"Abner's idea. He dragged me out of the house."

I looked at Abner. His eyes were bright, the way they always got when he had a choice bit of news or gossip to tell. He said, "Fella from Los Angeles went and bought Smuggler's Island. Can you beat that?"

"Bought it?" I said. "You mean outright?"

"Yep. Paid the county a hundred thousand cash."

"How'd you hear about it?"

"Jack Kewin, over to the real estate office."

"Who's the fellow who bought it?"

"Name's Roger Vauclain," Abner said. "Jack don't know any more about him. Did the buying through an agent."

Davey said, "Wonder what he wants with it?"

"Maybe he's got ideas of hunting treasure," Abner said, and winked at him. "Maybe he heard about what's hidden in those caves."

172

Pa gave him a look. "Old fool," he said.

Davey grinned, and I smiled a little and turned to look to where Smuggler's Island sat wreathed in fog half a mile straight out across the choppy harbor. It wasn't much to look at, from a distance or up close. Just one big oblong chunk of eroded rock about an acre and a half in size surrounded by a lot of little islets. It had a few stunted trees and shrubs, and a long headland where gulls built their nests, and a sheltered cover on the lee shore where you could put in a small boat. That was about all there was to it – except for those caves Abner had spoken of.

They were located near the lee cover and you could only get into them at low tide. Some said caves honeycombed the whole underbelly of the island, but those of us who'd ignored warnings from our parents as kids and gone exploring in them knew that this wasn't so. There were three caves and two of them had branches that led deep into the rock, but all of the tunnels were dead ends.

This business of treasure being hidden in one of those caves was just so much nonsense, of course – sort of a local legend that nobody took seriously. What the treasure was supposed to be was two million dollars in greenbacks that had been hidden by a rackets courier during Prohibition, when he'd been chased to the island by a team of Revenue agents. There was also supposed to be fifty cases of high-grade moonshine secreted there.

The bootlegging part of it had a good deal of truth, though. This section of the Northern California coast was a hotbed of illegal liquor traffic in the days of the Volstead Act, and the scene of several confrontations between smugglers and Revenue agents; half a dozen men on both sides had been killed, or had turned up missing and presumed dead. The way the bootleggers worked was to bring ships down from Canada outfitted as distilleries – big stills in their holds, bottling equipment, labels for a dozen different kinds of Canadian whisky – and anchor them twenty-five miles offshore. Then local fishermen and imported hirelings would go out in their boats and carry the liquor to places along the shore, where trucks would be waiting to pick it up and transport it down to San Francisco or east into Nevada. Smuggler's Island was supposed to have been a short-term storage point for whisky that couldn't be trucked out right away, which may or may not have been a true fact. At any rate, that was how the island got its name.

Just as I turned back to Pa and Abner, Handy came out of the processing shed with the tally clerk and the scales. He was a big, thick-necked man, Handy, with red hair and temper to match; he was also one of the best mates around and knew as much about salmon trolling and diesel engines as anybody in Camaroon Bay. He'd been working for me eight years, but he wouldn't be much longer. He was saving up to buy a boat of his own and only needed another thousand or so to swing the down payment.

Abner told him right away about this Roger Vauclain buying Smuggler's Island. Handy grunted and said, "Anybody that'd want those rocks out there has to have rocks in his head."

"Who do you imagine he is?" Davey asked.

"One of those damn-fool rich people probably," Pa said. "Buy something for no good reason except that it's there and they want it."

"But why Smuggler's Island in particular?"

"Got a fancy name, that's why. Now he can say to his friends, why look here, I own a place up north called Smuggler's Island, supposed to have treasure hidden on it."

I said, "Well, whoever he is and whyever
175

he bought it, we'll find out eventually. Right now we've got a catch to unload."

"Sure is a puzzler though, ain't it, Verne?" Abner said.

"It is that," I admitted. "It's a puzzler, all right."

If you live in a small town or village, you know how it is when something happens that has no immediate explanation. Rumors start flying, based on few or no facts, and every time one of them is retold to somebody else it gets exaggerated. Nothing much goes on in a place like Camaroon Bay anyhow – conversation is pretty much limited to the weather and the actions of tourists and how the salmon are running or how the crabs seem to be thinning out a little more every year. So this Roger Vauclain buying Smuggler's Island got a lot more lip service paid to it than it would have someplace else.

Jack Kewin didn't find out much about Vauclain, just that he was some kind of wealthy resident of Southern California. But that was enough for the speculations and the rumors to build on. During the next week I heard from different people that Vauclain was a real estate speculator who was going to construct a small private club on the island; that he was a retired bootlegger who'd worked the coast during Prohibition and had bought the island for nostalgic reasons; that he was a front man for a movie company that was going to film a big spectacular in Camaroon Bay and blow up the island in the final scene. None of these rumors made much sense, but that didn't stop people from spreading them and half-believing in them.

Then, one night while we were eating supper, Abner came knocking at the front door of our house on the hill above the village. Davey went and let him in, and he sat down at the table next to Pa. One look at him was enough to tell us that he'd come with news.

"Just been talking to Lloyd Simms," he said as Jennie poured him a cup of coffee. "Who do you reckon just made a reservation at the Camaroon Inn?"

"Who?" I asked.

"Roger Vauclain himself. Lloyd talked to him on the phone less than an hour ago, says he sounded pretty hard-nosed. Booked a single room for a week, be here on Thursday."

"Only a single room?" Jennie said. "Why, I'm disappointed, Abner. I expected he'd be traveling with an entourage." She's a practical woman and when it comes to things she considers nonsense, like all the hoopla

177

over Vauclain and Smuggler's Island, her sense of humor sharpens into sarcasm.

"Might be others coming up later," Abner said seriously.

Davey said, "Week's a long time for a rich man to spend in a place like Camaroon Bay. I wonder what he figures to do all that time?"

"Tend to his island, probably," I said.

"Tend to it?" Pa said. "Tend to what? You can walk over the whole thing in two hours."

"Well, there's always the caves, Pa."

He snorted. "Grown man'd have to be a fool to go wandering in those caves. Tide comes in while he's inside, he'll drown for sure."

"What time's he due in on Thursday?" Davey asked Abner.

"Around noon, Lloyd says. Reckon we'll find out then what he's planning to do with the island."

"Not planning to do anything with it, I tell you," Pa said. "Just wants to *own* it."

"We'll see," Abner said. "We'll see."

Thursday was clear and warm, and it should have been a good day for salmon; but maybe the run had started to peter out because it took us until almost noon to make the limit.

It was after two o'clock before we got the catch unloaded and weighed in at Bay Fisheries. Davey had some errands to run, and Handy had logged enough extra time, so I took the *Jennie Too* over to the commercial slips myself and stayed aboard her to hose down the decks. When I was through with that, I set about replacing the port outrigger line because it had started to weaken and we'd been having trouble with it.

I was doing that when a tall man came down the ramp from the quay and stood just off the bow, watching me. I didn't pay much attention to him; tourists stop by to rubberneck now and then, and if you encourage them they sometimes hang around so you can't get any work done. But then this fellow slapped a hand against his leg, as if he were annoyed, and called out in a loud voice, "Hey, you there. Fisherman."

I looked at him then, frowning. I'd heard that tone before: sharp, full of self-granted authority. Some city people are like that; to them, anybody who lives in a rural village is a low-class hick. I didn't like it and I let him see that in my face. "You talking to me?"

"Who else would I be talking to?"

I didn't say anything. He was in his forties, smooth-looking, and dressed in white ducks and a crisp blue windbreaker. If nothing else, his eyes were enough to make you dislike him immediately; they were hard and unfriendly and said that he was used to getting his own way.

He said, "Where can I rent a boat?"

"What kind of boat? To go sportfishing?"

"No, not to go sportfishing. A small cruiser."

"There ain't any cruisers for rent here."

He made a disgusted sound, as if he'd expected that. "A big outboard then," he said. "Something seaworthy."

"It's not a good idea to take a small boat out of the harbor," I said. "The ocean along here is pretty rough –"

"I don't want advice," he said. "I want a boat big enough to get me out to Smuggler's Island and back. Now who do I see about it?"

"Smuggler's Island?" I looked at him more closely. "Your name happen to be Roger Vauclain, by any chance?"

"That's right. You heard about me buying the island, I suppose. Along with everybody else in this place."

"News gets around," I said mildly.

"About that boat," he said.

"Talk to Ed Hawkins at Bay Marine on the wharf. He'll find something for you."

Vauclain gave me a curt nod and started to turn away.

I said, "Mind if I ask *you* a question now?"

He turned back. "What is it?"

"People don't go buying islands very often," I said, "particularly one like Smuggler's. I'd be interested to know your plans for it."

"You and every other damned person in Camaroon Bay."

I held my temper. "I was just asking. You don't have to give me an answer."

He was silent for a moment. Then he said, "What the hell, it's no secret. I've always wanted to live on an island, and that one out there is the only one around I can afford."

I stared at him. "You mean you're going to *build* on it?"

"That surprises you, does it?"

"It does," I said. "There's nothing on Smuggler's Island but rocks and a few trees and a couple of thousand nesting gulls. It's fogbound most of the time, and even when it's not, the wind blows at thirty knots or better."

"I like fog and wind and ocean," Vauclain said. "I like isolation. I don't like people much. That satisfy you?"

I shrugged. "To each his own."

181

"Exactly," he said, and went away up the ramp.

I worked on the *Jennie Too* another hour, then I went over to the Wharf Cafe for a cup of coffee and a piece of pie. When I came inside I saw Pa, Abner, and Handy sitting at one of the copper-topped tables. I walked over to them.

They already knew that Vauclain had arrived in Camaroon Bay. Handy was saying, "Hell, he's about as friendly as a shark. I was over to Ed Hawkins' place shooting the breeze when he came in and demanded Ed get him a boat. Threw his weight around for fifteen minutes until Ed agreed to rent him his own Chris-Craft. Then he paid for the rental in cash, slammed two fifties on Ed's desk like they were singles and Ed was a beggar."

I sat down. "He's an eccentric, all right," I said. "I talked to him for a few minutes myself about an hour ago."

"Eccentric?" Abner said, and snorted. "That's just a name they give to people who never learned manners or good sense."

Pa said to me, "He tell you what he's fixing to do with Smuggler's Island, Verne?"

"He did, yep."

"Told Abner too, over to the Inn." Pa shook his head, glowering, and lighted a
182

pipe. "Craziest damned thing I ever heard. Build a house on that mess of rock, live out there. Crazy, that's all."

"That's a fact," Handy said. "I'd give him more credit if he was planning to hunt for that bootlegger's treasure."

"Well, I'm sure not going to relish having him for a neighbor," Abner said. "Don't guess anybody else will, either."

None of us disagreed with that. A man likes to be able to get along with his neighbors, rich or poor. Getting along with Vauclain, it seemed, was going to be a chore for everybody.

In the next couple of days Vauclain didn't do much to improve his standing with the residents of Camaroon Bay. He snapped at merchants and waitresses, ignored anybody who tried to strike up a conversation with him, and complained twice to Lloyd Simms about the service at the Inn. The only good thing about him, most people were saying, was that he spent the better part of his days on Smuggler's Island – doing what, nobody knew exactly – and his nights locked in his room. Might have been he was drawing up plans there for the house he intended to build on the island.

Rumor now had it that Vauclain was an

architect, one of these independents who'd built up a reputation, like Frank Lloyd Wright in the old days, and who only worked for private individuals and companies. This was probably true since it originated with Jack Kewin; he'd spent a little time with Vauclain and wasn't one to spread unfounded gossip. According to Jack, Vauclain had learned that the island was for sale more than six months ago and had been up twice before by helicopter from San Francisco to get an aerial view of it.

That was the way things stood on Sunday morning, when Jennie and I left for church at ten. Afterward we had lunch at a place up the coast, and then, because the weather was cool but still clear, we went for a drive through the redwood country. It was almost five when we got back home.

Pa was in bed – his lumbago was bothering him, he said – and Davey was gone somewhere. I went into our bedroom to change out of my suit. While I was in there, the telephone rang, and Jennie called out that it was for me.

When I picked up the receiver Lloyd Simms's voice said, "Sorry to bother you, Verne, but if you're not busy I need a favor."

"I'm not busy, Lloyd. What is it?"

"Well, it's Roger Vauclain. He went out

to the island this morning like usual, and he was supposed to be back at three to take a telephone call. Told me to make sure I was around then, the call was important – you know the way he talks. The call came in right on schedule, but Vauclain didn't. He's still not back, and the party calling him has been ringing me up every half hour, demanding I get hold of him. Something about a bid that has to be delivered first thing tomorrow morning."

"You want me to go out to the island, Lloyd?"

"If you wouldn't mind," he said. "I don't much care about Vauclain, the way he's been acting, but this caller is driving me up a wall. And it could be something's the matter with Vauclain's boat; can't get it started or something. Seems kind of funny he didn't come back when he said he would."

I hesitated. I didn't much want to take the time to go out to Smuggler's Island; but then if there was a chance Vauclain was in trouble I couldn't very well refuse to help.

"All right," I said. "I'll see what I can do."

We rang off, and I explained to Jennie where I was going and why. Then I drove down to the basin where the pleasure-boat slips were and took the tarp off Davey's sixteen-foot Sportliner inboard. I'd bought it for him on his sixteenth birthday, when I figured he was old enough to handle a small boat of his own, but I used it as much as he did. We're not so well off that we can afford to keep more than one pleasure craft.

The engine started right up for a change – usually you have to choke it several times on cool days – and I took her out of the slips and into the harbor. The sun was hidden by overcast now and the wind was up, building small whitecaps, running fogbanks in from the ocean but shredding them before they reached the shore. I followed the south jetty out past the breakwater and into open sea. The water was choppier there, the color of gunmetal, and the wind was pretty cold; I pulled the collar of my jacket up and put on my gloves to keep my hands from numbing on the wheel.

When I neared the island, I swung around to the north shore and into the lee cove. Ed Hawkins' Chris-Craft was tied up there all right, bow and stern lines made fast to outcroppings on a long, natural stone dock. I took the Sportliner in behind it, climbed out onto the bare rock, and made her fast. On my right, waves broke over and into the mouths of the three caves, hissing long fans of spray. Gulls wheeled screeching above the

186

headland; farther in, scrub oak and cypress danced like line bobbers in the wind. It all made you feel as though you were standing on the edge of the world.

There was no sign of Vauclain anywhere at the cove, so I went up through a tangle of artichoke plants toward the center of the island. The area there was rocky but mostly flat, dotted with undergrowth and patches of sandy earth. I stopped beside a gnarled cypress and scanned from left to right. Nothing but emptiness. Then I walked out toward the headland, hunched over against the pull of the wind. But I didn't find him there, either.

A sudden thought came to me as I started back and the hairs prickled on my neck. What if he'd gone into the caves and been trapped there when the tide began to flood? If that was what had happened, it was too late for me to do anything – but I started to run anyway, my eyes on the ground so I wouldn't trip over a bush or a rock.

I was almost back to the cove, coming at a different angle from before, when I saw him.

It was so unexpected that I pulled up short and almost lost my footing on loose rock. The pit of my stomach went hollow. He was lying on his back in a bed of artichokes, one arm flung out and the other wrapped across his chest. There was blood under his arm, and blood spread across the front of his windbreaker. One long look was all I needed to tell me he'd been shot and that he was dead.

Shock and an eerie sense of unreality kept me standing there another few seconds. My thoughts were jumbled; you don't think too clearly when you stumble on a dead man, a murdered man. And it *was* murder, I knew that well enough. There was no gun anywhere near the body, and no way it could have been an accident.

Then I turned, shivering, and ran down to the cove and took the Sportliner away from there at full throttle to call for the county sheriff.

Vauclain's death was the biggest event that had happened in Camaroon Bay in forty years, and Sunday night and Monday nobody talked about anything else. As soon as word got around that I was the one who'd discovered the body, the doorbell and the telephone didn't stop ringing – friends and neighbors, newspaper people, investigators. The only place I had any peace was on the *Jennie Too* Monday morning, and not much there because Davey and Handy wouldn't let the subject alone while we fished.

188

By late that afternoon the authorities had questioned just about everyone in the area. It didn't appear they'd found out anything, though. Vauclain had been alone when he'd left for the island early Sunday; Abner had been down at the slips then and swore to the fact. A couple of tourists had rented boats from Ed Hawkins during the day, since the weather was pretty good, and a lot of locals were out in the harbor on pleasure craft. But whoever it was who had gone to Smuggler's Island after Vauclain, he hadn't been noticed.

As to a motive for the shooting, there were all sorts of wild speculations. Vauclain had wronged somebody in Los Angeles and that person had followed him here to take revenge. He'd treated a local citizen badly enough to trigger a murderous rage. He'd gotten in bad with organized crime and a contract had been put out on him. And the most farfetched theory of all: he'd actually uncovered some sort of treasure on Smuggler's Island and somebody'd learned about it and killed him for it. But the simple truth was, nobody had *any* idea why Vauclain was murdered. If the sheriff's department had found any clues on the island or anywhere else, they weren't talking – but they weren't making any arrests, either.

There was a lot of excitement, all right. Only, underneath it all people were nervous and a little scared. A killer seemed to be loose in Camaroon Bay, and if he'd murdered once, who was to say he wouldn't do it again? A mystery is all well and good when it's happening someplace else, but when it's right on your doorstep you can't help but feel threatened and apprehensive.

I'd had about all the pestering I could stand by four o'clock, so I got into the car and drove up the coast to Shelter Cove. That gave me an hour's worth of freedom. But no sooner did I get back to Camaroon Bay, with the intention of going home and locking myself in my basement workshop, than a sheriff's cruiser pulled up behind me at a stop sign and its horn started honking. I sighed and pulled over to the curb.

It was Harry Swenson, one of the deputies who'd questioned me the day before, after I'd reported finding Vauclain's body. We knew each other well enough to be on a first name basis. He said, "Verne, the sheriff asked me to talk to you again, see if there's anything you might have overlooked yesterday. You mind?"

"No, I don't mind," I said tiredly.

We went into the Inn and took a table at the back of the dining room. A couple of people stared at us, and I could see Lloyd Simms hovering around out by the front desk. I wondered how long it would be before I'd stop being the center of attention every time I went someplace in the village.

Over coffee, I repeated everything that had happened Sunday afternoon. Harry checked what I said with notes he'd taken; then he shook his head and closed the notebook.

"Didn't really expect you to remember anything else," he said, "but we had to make sure. Truth is, Verne, we're up against it on this thing. Damnedest case I ever saw."

"Guess that means you haven't found out anything positive."

"Not much. If we could figure a motive, we might be able to get a handle on it from that. But we just can't find one."

I decided to give voice to one of my own theories. "What about robbery, Harry?" I asked. "Seems I heard Vauclain was carrying a lot of cash with him and throwing it around pretty freely."

"We thought of that first thing," he said. "No good, though. His wallet was on the body, and there was three hundred dollars in it and a couple of blank checks."

I frowned down at my coffee. "I don't like to say this, but you don't suppose it could be one of these thrill killings we're always reading about?"

"Man, I hope not. That's the worst kind of homicide there is."

We were silent for a minute or so. Then I said, "You find anything at all on the island? Any clues?"

He hesitated. "Well," he said finally, "I probably shouldn't discuss it – but then, you're not the sort to break a confidence. We did find one thing near the body. Might not mean anything, but it's not the kind of item you'd expect to come across out there."

"What is it?"

"A cake of white beeswax," he said.

"Beeswax?"

"Right. Small cake of it. Suggest anything to you?"

"No," I said. "No, nothing."

"Not to us either. Aside from that, we haven't got a thing. Like I said, we're up against it. Unless we get a break in the next couple of days, I'm afraid the whole business will end up in the unsolved file – that's unofficial, now."

"Sure," I said.

Harry finished his coffee. "I'd better get moving," he said. "Thanks for your time, Verne."

I nodded, and he stood up and walked out

across the dining room. As soon as he was gone, Lloyd came over and wanted to know what we'd been talking about. But I'd begun to feel oddly nervous all of a sudden, and there was something tickling at the edge of my mind. I cut him off short, saying, "Let me be, will you, Lloyd? Just let me be for a minute."

When he drifted off, looking hurt, I sat there and rotated my cup on the table. Beeswax, I thought. I'd told Harry that it didn't suggest anything to me, and yet it did, vaguely. Beeswax. White beeswax . . .

It came to me then – and along with it a couple of other things, little things, like missing figures in an arithmetic problem. I went cold all over, as if somebody had opened a window and let the wind inside the room. I told myself I was wrong, but it couldn't be. But I wasn't wrong. It made me sick inside, but I wasn't wrong.

I knew who had murdered Roger Vauclain.

When I came into the house I saw him sitting out on the sun deck, just sitting there motionless with his hands flat on his knees, staring out to sea. Or out to where Smuggler's Island sat shining hard and ugly in the glare of the dying sun.

I didn't go out there right away. First I went into the other rooms to see if anybody else was home, but nobody was. Then, when I couldn't put it off any longer, I got myself ready to face it and walked onto the deck.

He glanced at me as I leaned back against the railing. I hadn't seen much of him since finding the body, or paid much attention to him when I had; but now I saw that his eyes looked different. They didn't blink. They looked at me, they looked past me, but they didn't blink.

"Why'd you do it, Pa?" I said. "Why'd you kill Vauclain?"

I don't know what I expected his reaction to be. But there wasn't any reaction. He wasn't startled, he wasn't frightened, he wasn't anything. He just looked away from me again and sat there like a man who has expected to hear the words for a long time.

I kept waiting for him to say something, to move, to blink his eyes. For one full minute and half of another, he did nothing. Then he sighed, soft and tired, and he said, "I knew somebody'd find out this time." His voice was steady, calm. "I'm sorry it had to be you, Verne."

"So am I."

"How'd you know?"

"You left a cake of white beeswax out

194

there," I said. "Fell out of your pocket when you pulled the gun, I guess. You're just the only person around here who'd be likely to have white beeswax in his pocket, Pa, because you're the only person who hand-carves his own meerschaum pipes. Took me a time to remember that you use wax like that to seal the bowls and give them a luster finish."

He didn't say anything.

"Couple of other things, too," I said. "You in bed yesterday when Jennie and I got home. It was a clear day, no early fog, nothing to aggravate your lumbago. Unless you'd been out someplace where you weren't protected from the wind – someplace like in a boat on open water. Then there was Davey's Sportliner starting right up for me. Almost never does that on cool days unless it's been run recently, and the only person besides Davey and me who has a key is you."

He nodded. "It's usually the little things," he said. "I always figured it'd be some little thing that'd finally do it."

"Pa," I said, "why'd you kill him?"

"He had to go and buy the island. Then he had to decide to build a house on it, I couldn't let him do that. I went out there to talk to him, try to get him to change his mind. Took my revolver along, but only just

195

in case; wasn't intending to use it. Only he wouldn't listen to me. Called me an old fool and worse, and then he give me a shove. He was dead before I knew it, seems like."

"What'd him building a house have to do with you?"

"He'd have brought men and equipment out there, wouldn't he? They'd have dug up everything, wouldn't they? They'd have sure dug up the Revenue man."

I thought he was rambling. "Pa . . ."

"You got a right to know about that, too," he said. He blinked then, four times fast. "In 1929 a fella named Frank Eberle and me went to work for the bootleggers. Hauling whisky. We'd go out maybe once a month in Frank's boat, me acting as shotgun, and we'd bring in a load of shine – mostly to Shelter Cove, but sometimes we'd be told to drop it off on Smuggler's for a day or two. It was easy money, and your ma and me needed it, what with you happening along, and what the hell, Frank always said, we were only helping to give the people what they wanted.

"But then one night in 1932 it all went bust. We brought a shipment to the island and just after we started unloading it this man run out of the trees waving a gun and yelling that we were under arrest. A Revenue

196

agent, been lying up there in ambush. Lying alone because he didn't figure to have much trouble, I reckon – and I found out later the government people had bigger fish to fry up to Shelter Cove that night.

"Soon as the agent showed himself, Frank panicked and started to run. Agent put a shot over his head, and before I could think on it, I cut loose with the rifle I always carried. I killed him, Verne, I shot that man dead."

He paused, his face twisting with memory. I wanted to say something – but what was there to say?

Pa said, "Frank and me buried him on the island, under a couple of rocks on the center flat. Then we got out of there. I quit the bootleggers right away, but Frank, he kept on with it and got himself killed in a big shootout up by Eureka just before Repeal. I knew they were going to get me too someday. Only time kept passing and somehow it never happened, and I almost had myself believing it never would. Then this Vauclain came along. You see now why I couldn't let him build his house?"

"Pa," I said thickly, "it's been forty-five years since all that happened. All anybody'd have dug up was bones. Maybe there's something there to identify the Revenue agent, but there couldn't be anything that'd point to you."

"Yes, there could," he said. "Just like there was something this time – the beeswax and all. There'd have been something, all right, and they'd have come for me."

He stopped talking then, abruptly, like a machine that had been turned off, and swiveled his head away and just sat staring again. There in the sun, I still felt cold. He believed what he'd just said; he honestly believed it.

I knew now why he'd been so dour and moody for most of my life, why he almost never smiled, why he'd never let me get close to him. And I knew something else, too: I wasn't going to tell the sheriff any of this. He was my father and he was seventy-two years old; and I'd see to it that he didn't hurt anybody else. But the main reason was, if I let it happen that they really did come for him he wouldn't last a month. In an awful kind of way the only thing that'd been holding him together all these years was his certainty they *would* come someday.

Besides, it didn't matter anyway. He hadn't actually gotten away with anything. He hadn't committed one unpunished murder, or now two unpunished murders, because there is no such thing. There's just no such thing as the perfect crime.

I walked over and took the chair beside him, and together we sat quiet and looked out at Smuggler's Island. Only I didn't see it very well because my eyes were full of tears.

Monkey King

by James Holding

I've always loved jade. Green jade refreshes
me like the cool crisp taste of mint in my
mouth. Pink jade reminds me of sunset cloud
that's been carved from the sky with a soft
knife. And white jade makes delicious icicles
of pleasure parade down my back like tiger
tracks in snow.

Indeed, I'm hardly normal when it comes
to jade; unfortunately, I've never had the
means to indulge my feeling for it. If I'd
been a millionaire, I'd have assembled a
private collection. If I'd had an adequate
education, I might have become an expert
on the subject, serving on the staff of a
distinguished museum. But as it is, forced
since childhood to scratch desperately for a
living, I'm a thief.

Not a common thief, however; I specialize
in jade. And by "jade" I mean not only
jadeite, nephrite and chlormelanite, the true
jade minerals, but all their beautiful blood
brothers, too, from saussearite to quartz.

200

That's what I was doing in Bangkok.

Bangkok is the home of the Green Monkey, an image of Hanuman, the ancient monkey king, lovingly carved five hundred years ago from a single block of flawless green Chanthaburi jasper. The head is thirty-five centimeters tall, the body gowned in rich vestments, seated on a golden pyramid-shaped throne twelve feet high, and proudly displayed in an exquisite temple-museum building of its own, just off the Royal Plaza. It's one of the loveliest jades in Asia.

I intended to steal it.

The round the world cruise ship, on which I'd been a minimum rate passenger since San Francisco, anchored at dawn off the mouth of the Chao Phraya River in the Gulf of Siam. A huge flat-bottom barge met it there to carry three hundred of us, American tourists all, across the sand bar blocking the river's mouth and upstream to Bangkok for two days of sightseeing, then back down-stream to our cruise ship again the next evening.

Incredibly, there was no customs in-spection for two-day cruise touring of our kind, either coming or going from Bangkok. That's why I chose to enter the city, and leave it, as such a tourist. For the excursion,

201

I carried with me from the ship only my large holdall camera bag, toothbrush and razor, and my umbrella.

Arriving in Bangkok, I left my fellow tourists to their own devices and took a taxi to the Ratanokosin Hotel where I registered. It's only two blocks from the Royal Plaza and the Abode of the Green Monkey. When the boy showed me to my room, I took off my jacket and tie, switched on the air conditioner to full, and ordered a gin sling sent up.

Sipping it in a positive glow of anticipation and pleasure, I went over my plans once more, carefully and professionally. They were simple in the extreme. I'd reconnoitered the job several months before, you understand. I knew what I was up against. No one would question my camera case, I was sure. In a city whose temples, canals and towers are so infinitely photogenic, photographers are as common as cockroaches in China. And certainly no one would suspect my umbrella, a common sight on the streets of Bangkok at the beginning of the rainy season.

This was Saturday afternoon. My real work didn't start until Sunday, since the Abode of the Green Monkey is open to the public only on Sundays.

On Sunday, I arose late to a muggy,

overcast day threatening rain. I felt fresh, confident, and strong. After a hearty breakfast at my hotel, I listened contentedly for an hour or so to the Sunday concert of music played on the *ranad ek,* or bamboo xylophone, by three Thais in the hotel lobby. Then I went to my room, secured my camera bag and umbrella, and checking the time carefully, set off for the Abode of the Green Monkey.

Under the wide overhang of its gracefully curved roof, the Abode's double doors are high and broad, beautifully inlaid with mother-of-pearl. They are guarded by an imposing pair of glazed tile demons, one on either side, and more effectively, perhaps, by half a dozen slightly-built Thai guards with ingratiating ways and fineboned faces, who patrol the platform outside while the Abode is open to the public.

The sweet tinkling notes of temple bells filled Bangkok's air, but I had ears and eyes for nothing save my immediate goal. And there it was. Dimly through the open doors I could see the Monkey King squatting crosslegged, wrinkled and benign atop his gold throne.

Scores of Bangkok residents and foreign tourists were streaming in and out of the great doors, even though it was now only five minutes until noon, when the Abode of the Green Monkey would be closed for the siesta hours. Casually I joined a spate of ingoing tourists, my camera draped around my neck in approved shutterbug style, my camera case hanging by its stout strap over my shoulder, my furled umbrella in my right hand. Soon I formed a part of a knot of sightseers who stood at the foot of the pyramidal throne and gazed upward, enthralled at the simian jade features of the Green Mountain which sat serenely above our heads on the pyramid's truncated top.

Unnoticed, I edged out of the cluster and around to the side of the throne, where I began to examine with spurious interest one of the lifesize golden statues that flank it. Shielded by this statue, I unslung my camera case and put it down as though to rest a moment. When no one was looking, I shoved the case out of sight with my foot under the trailing skirt of gold brocade that hangs down to the floor on all sides of the throne to mask the lower beams of its inner framework. It was the place I had selected, after much observation on my previous visit.

Nobody took any notice of me. I wandered farther toward the rear of the throne, glancing at my watch. A moment later I heard the voices of the guards outside the doors calling out that it was closing time; the tourists and sightseers rapidly began to depart. When I felt safe from observation, one minute before the noon closing hour by my watch, I lay down on the floor behind the throne, lifting its brocade skirt, and rolled under the platform with my umbrella, all in one smooth uninterrupted flow of silent motion. I dropped the brocade skirt back in place, and grinned with delight.

I was completely concealed. Seconds later, two guards made a circuit of the Abode's interior to check that all visitors had left before they locked the massive doors. I could hear their heels clicking on the floor. And although their inspection of the premises was superficial at best, I was glad I was well hidden. If I could get past this tense moment without discovery, if the guards who saw me come in had not remarked my absence in the flow of departing visitors, I was home free. The guards were changed for the afternoon shift, I knew. There would be new men outside when I left with the Green Monkey.

With my ear to the marble floor, I heard the jarring thuds that told me the massive doors had been swung shut. Darkness and silence descended on me as the dim lights were switched off from outside.

I waited several minutes. Then I rolled out

from under the throne, groped in the blackness until I located my camera case, and drew it forth. From it, I took a flashlight which I lit and set upon the floor to work by. I unscrewed the cap from the end of my umbrella's fat, straight, outsized handle, and shook out of it a heavy cylinder of short, hollow, paper-thin steel tubes, nested one inside the other for storage, but capable of being screwed together like the sections of a fishing rod to form a light, strong ladder. I was proud of that ladder when it stood assembled less than fifteen minutes later. I'd designed it myself, and the oversized umbrella shaft and handle, too.

I was prouder still of the next object I lifted from my camera holdall bag. It was the heart and soul of my plan for stealing the Green Monkey.

Have you ever been in a glass factory? And seen the solid, rough-hewn chunks of broken green glass called "cullet" that they take out of the bed of a glass furnace when they shut the furnace down to reline it with new fire brick? Maybe you haven't. But what I took from my case in the Abode of the Green Monkey that day was just such a chunk of cullet, roughly pyramidal in shape, and like no other chunk of cullet in one respect: its upper section had been crudely carved and ground into a recognizable monkey's head.

It was, indeed, my first attempt at sculpture and not too badly done, I told myself. I had stolen the chunk of cullet from the waste pile of a California factory; I had lovingly worked on it in my cabin for five long weeks of cruising, chipping, carving, rubbing it with fine sand to kill the gleam of glass.

I set it gently on the floor. I leaned on the ladder against the high throne of the Monkey King and flashlight in hand, climbed carefully upward. When I was high enough to reach the image, I took the flashlight between my teeth and used both hands to lift the Green Monkey from his pedestal. Then I carried him, still wearing his rich vestments, down the ladder to the floor, rung by precarious rung. There, I stripped his raiment from him, a royal headdress and a jewel-studded, stolelike cloak that entirely covered his body. I placed the headdress on my glass monkey's head, the concealing cloak around the shapeless torso of my chunk of cullet.

Examining the result in my flashlight's beam, I smiled to myself, not unsatisfied. Swathed as it was in cloak and headdress, the cullet looked enough like the Green Monkey to be his cousin, certainly enough to escape detection almost indefinitely in the anemic light of the Abode, perched so high above its viewers' heads.

Now I mounted my ladder once again and placed the glass statue on the Green Monkey's throne. I dismantled and restowed the ladder in my umbrella shaft. Then and only then, I turned the flashlight on the genuine jade image, now resting naked on the floor.

I caught my breath at its beauty. I devoured it with my eyes. I stroked it with tender fingertips. I rubbed my cheek against it. I did a slow blind dance with it in my arms, fondling it. The Green Monkey was mine.

At last, regretfully, I slid him out of sight into my camera bag where the chunk of cullet had nested until now. I zipped the case closed, then sat down to wait behind the throne in the darkness until the Abode of the Green Monkey should reopen for the afternoon.

I had much to think about. The time passed quickly. About ten minutes before the Abode reopened, a drumming, rushing sound began on the roof above me, and I correctly deduced it had begun to rain outside. Soon the lights inside my sanctum flashed on and the doors were thrown wide to the afternoon visitors.

Despite the rain, they arrived and entered in impressive numbers, quieting the only small worry I had – that if the shrine were sparsely patronized, I might have trouble departing it inconspicuously. I drifted aimlessly from the back of the throne, and managed to melt unnoticed into a group of tourists. I accompanied them when they left, secretly smiling to hear them enthuse over the piece of broken glass they thought was the Green Monkey.

Outside the doors under the roof's overhang, I saw it was raining very hard. All the better, I thought with delight. I raised my umbrella, like most of my companion tourists, and prepared to step out into the rain, the jade image of Hanuman, the Monkey King, safe in my camera bag, which was now all but concealed from view by my opened umbrella.

The Thai museum guards, clad in oilskin rain gear, still patrolled before the entrance doors, keeping a sharp eye on the crowd. They were different men from the morning's guard. I was safe.

During the brief moment I paused under the Abode's eaves, while I was opening my umbrella and savoring my triumph, I found time to pity those guards. They saw the statue of the Green Monkey every Sunday of their lives, true. But had they ever seen the Green Monkey unclothed, as I had, the glory of the jade unhidden? Had they ever felt the cool, faintly oily tenderness of the stone? Had they ever seen the unbelievable beauty of a flashlight's beam shining through the green translucence of the loveliest carved wonder in Asia? No. Poor bodyguards to the Monkey King, they were bodyguards only, and nothing more.

At the moment, the eyes of one of them scanned me, poised to step out into the rain, and the weird conviction swept through me that he was reading my thoughts across twenty feet of space.

For he frowned suddenly, and began to walk toward me, his intent gaze never leaving me for an instant. At the same time, he made a sign to two other guards nearby who immediately began to converge upon me. Within the space of a single breath, all three stood confronting me, looking ridiculously petite in their little oilskins but somehow threatening, too, with the rain dripping from their hats, noses, and chins.

"*Kho apia,*" said the first one, politely. Then he switched to English. "Pardon, sir. Will you come with us, please?"

210

I gaped at him, utterly confounded. "Why?"

"Cannot talk in rain," he said. "Kindly accompany us in car, yes?" He was very apologetic, but also very stern, very sincere.

"Accompany you? In a car? Are you crazy?" I bleated. A spasm of genuine alarm squeezed my heart. I peered at him under the rim of my umbrella.

The other two guards stepped close and placed delicate hands gently on each of my arms. "Come," said my thought-reader, and led the way toward the car park beside the street.

My heart dropped into my shoes. As I followed between my captors, the camera bag over my shoulder suddenly seemed intolerably heavy, as though the Monkey King weighed a million pounds.

They took me to police headquarters, where a doll-like magistrate listened to a rapid flood of Thai from my guards, punctuated with thumb-jerking in my direction. Then, at a crisp command from the magistrate, I was relieved of my passport, camera case, and umbrella. They found the Monkey King within seconds.

I was locked into a cell, still dazed and uncomprehending. I had been promptly arrested after a single casual glance from the

211

guard. Why? Everything had gone so smoothly, so swimmingly. Nothing, I told myself stubbornly, *nothing* could possibly have given me away, so it must have been thought-reading or some other occult art that had brought the gendarmes down on me. Orientals sometimes possess strange mental powers, they say.

Through the bars of my cell door, I said to the English-speaking guard who was locking me in, "Tell me, please, how did you know I had stolen the Monkey King?" I had been caught with the goods – there was no use pretending innocence.

He looked at me, smiling. "You inside Abode of Hanuman alone during siesta," he lisped. "This very suspicious, no?"

"Very suspicious, yes. But how did you *know* I'd been inside during siesta, just by looking at me?"

He shrugged daintily. "Rain," he said.

"Rain? What's that got to do with it?"

"Rain begin before opening of Abode for afternoon, yes?"

I nodded.

"That explain mystery, sir," he said. "Very sorry." He went away.

Belatedly, then, the light dawned on me.

My umbrella had been *dry* when I raised it to leave the Abode of the Monkey King.

Nice Work If You Can Get It

by Donald Honig

The threat of competition, an ugly noise that generally starts when your back is turned, can waken a man's pride and arouse his self-respect until it glitters like the eye of a tiger. Competition is a disease that sooner or later infects every trade and profession and makes it take a long step forward. Still, it remains the obligation of every honorable man to oppose it with all his skills.

As a matter of record, me and my associates, Jack and Buck, have long been the leading exponents of the delicate art of scoop-'em-up, which is the art of abduction fined down to a science whereby not a footprint, fingerprint, howl, yelp, or regret is left behind. Perfection is the only formula for success in this tricky profession. Tyros have long studied our techniques and have tried, with no luck, to emulate them.

So I was quite surprised to hear one day that another organization had scraped up the

213

men, the courage, and the resources to go into competition with us. I met the captain of the crew one afternoon while paying my semi-annual visit to my aged father (a retired second story man who had developed vertigo) at the Home for Retired Vikings, which is a fine old institution maintained by the trade, catering to sore-footed footpads, conscience-stricken swindlers, abstemious rum runners, arthritic forgers, and cattle thieves turned vegetarian.

On the way back to the bus I chanced to run into Barney Blue, an old friend from bars both legal and alcoholic. Barney had been visiting his father, an old safecracker who had been forced into premature retirement after developing an unaccountable fear of the dark.

"Bush," said Barney to me as we headed for the bus, "I have long admired your organization. You and your boys have stood pre-eminent and par-excellent in the field for years. Your capers have captured the hearts of bold men everywhere and become veritable textbooks on the art. I know all this because I've been studying them for years. Now, having learned the craft from the master, I've organized a little group of my own and we're going into competition with you."

"We're a nation of free enterprise, Barney," I said. "There's nothing wrong with you going into business for yourself, but I ought to warn you that you'll be doing yourself a severe disservice by announcing yourself as a competitor. You're encroaching on very, very private ground. Why try and buck perfection? Why don't you take your boys and go into something that calls for initiative, like holding up stagecoaches or selling protection to the vendors on the Oregon Trail?"

He laughed; but it was a terse sound.

"Don't like the idea of somebody coming into your pasture, eh, Bush?" he said. "Well, maybe the profession can stand a little more dash and daring. The talk is that you and your boys have become a bit smug and conservative lately. The grapes are withering on your vine, old boy," he said.

Well, I laughed him off gently. But when I returned home I found myself brooding a bit. Perhaps it *was* true that we had been doing some laurel-resting of late. I felt that we were on top and could afford to coast. But now this threat of competition cast a new light on everything. It was just possible that Barney Blue and his boys could score some tremendous coup and put us in the background. I decided there was but one thing to do: give my career a fresh crown. So I gathered together the boys and let them know.

"In order to repel this dreary threat," I said to Buck and Jack, "we have to perform a job which for skill and audacity, will belittle anything that Barney Blue and his boys can conceive, as well as make all our previous efforts look like blueprints. We have to swing a job that will gladden every heart in the Home for Retired Vikings, give inspiration to novices and hope to failures, as well as teach an enduring lesson to Barney Blue and his boys." And I meant *enduring*.

"It sounds big," said Jack.

"It will have to be big," I said. "It can be nothing less than the greatest scoop job in history. I want a job of such magnitude that it will bathe our competitors in shame, of such brilliance that historians the world over will skip a hundred pages in their manuscripts and begin recording us in the next century."

Jack beamed happily; the boys had an ardent and spirited attitude in these matters. Big Buck remained sullen, but I could tell that even he was inspired.

"Who do you have in mind as a subject, Bush?" Jack asked.

"See if you can guess: who is the richest man in the world?"

"Not him," said Jack, shocked.

"Yes, him," I said.

"But it's practically impossible to get near him," Jack said. "He's only too well aware of people like us. His car is a tank and his bodyguards are Neanderthals."

"Those are his achievements," I said. "He also has his weak points. He's impressed and disarmed by millionaires and other dubious celebrities."

"Who are we talking about?" Buck asked, making a rare utterance. He was strictly brawn.

"J. J. Griggen, the bilious billionaire," I said.

"The oil man," Jack said.

"Yes," I said, "oil. Whenever any thing in the world stops, stalls, or squeaks, it's another windfall for J. J. Griggen."

"He sounds likely," Buck said.

"We can ask five million for him," I said. "And get it. We'd be depriving him of a week's salary, but what of it. He'll buy up a few congressmen, have them put through a ransom-is-deductible law, and then forget about the whole thing."

"But how do you make the scoop?" Jack asked.

"I've got that worked out," I said. "Barney Blue's audacious intrusion upon our personal domain has inspired me to conceive the noblest attempt of our career. J. J. Griggen is going to attend a Charity Ball for Overprivileged Children two weeks from tonight. The ball is being held in order to raise funds to build mosaic handball courts for these kids in their Adirondack summer retreats. And the enchanting thing is it's going to be a masquerade ball. It was in the papers today. Boys," I said, "pick out your costumes, unbutton your alter egos, and let your hearts sing out – for we're going to a ball!"

From Handy Harry, the corner forger, we obtained our invitations to the ball. It was being primed as the social event of the season, and little did the primers know how eventful it was going to be. The affair was going to be held at one of those commodious Long Island mansions where they play polo in the living room on rainy days. We drove out there several times to inspect the premises, then back to the city to formulate the plan, which, as it took shape, was by turn feasible, infallible, ingenious, and diabolic.

I chose the costumes for my entourage. Buck was going to go as a caveman, *Homo extinctus,* with loincloth, club, and scowl.

Jack was going to be Lord Byron, with frills and ruffles and pithy couplets. I was going to be Millard Fillmore, dignified and undistinguished. And with us we were bringing an added, unannounced guest who was going to play an important role later in the evening.

We arrived at the ball at about nine thirty. The place was ablaze with lights and jewels. They were all there, dukes and duchesses and princes and princesses from places that are remembered today only by stamp collectors and retired map-makers; and all the playboys and tycoons and titans, and the men who live in Wall Street's shadow and the women who shadow Wall Street's men. All of them in costume. The grand ballroom was a whirl of bizarre celebrities. I shook hands with Oliver Cromwell, Talleyrand, William McKinley (there were three of them), Julius Caesar, Beau Brummel, Marie Antoinette, Madame Du Barry and dozens of others.

After an hour or so of calculated mingling, I finally caught sight of J. J. Griggen. Humble man that he was, he had come as Moses; not Michelangelo's Moses, but Griggen's Moses, short and paunchy and ferret-eyed. He might have been the real article, the way everyone stepped aside for him and stared after him.

I jostled him at the punch table.

"Excuse me, Moses," I said, and he laughed. He liked that.

"So you recognized me, eh?" he said.

"It was easy."

"And who might you be?" he asked.

"President Millard Fillmore," I said.

"President of what? G.M.?"

"U.S."

"Ah, Steel!" he said and graciously patted me on the back. "Always a pleasure, always a pleasure. Are you really in steel, sir?"

"In a way, if you want to say it's a play on words."

We talked, and while I beguiled the old boy with anecdotes, I was maneuvering him out onto a balcony. Outside, on the balcony, out of sight, we met a caveman. With a club.

"Ah," said Griggen with a laugh, "a representative of Organized Labor!" He offered to shake hands. But this caveman was not one for social niceties. One tap with the club and J. J. Griggen was stretched out on the balcony.

Then we went to work. Buck retrieved the parcel we had cached there, containing the unannounced guest – a bearskin which we had bought from a store that sells bearskins and halberds and morions and shrunken heads and Minié balls from the Gettysburg battlefield. While I propped up old J. J., Buck fitted him into the bearskin and zipped him up. Then Buck hefted the bear into his arms and I led them back into the ballroom.

"Thomas Jefferson," I announced to all the smiling, costumed guests, "leading behind me the symbolic brawn and brute strength of America." Several men, Lewis and Clark particularly, cheered, while a woman said how cunning it was.

I led the symbols out the front door and down the path to the parking lot. There I found Lord Byron at the wheel of our car, the motor running, the back door open. Buck dropped the bear onto the back seat and got in beside it. Then we took off down the driveway and through the gate where the special police in charge there for the evening saluted us nicely; after all, it wasn't every night they saw Millard Fillmore, Lord Byron, a caveman and the world's richest bear.

We sped along the dark, woodsy Long Island lanes, towards the little cabin I had prepared, up a dirt road, perfectly secluded. While it wasn't one of the great mansions that Griggen was accustomed to, he was going to have to call it home for the next few days.

By the time we pulled up to the place in

dark, warm, crickety night, Griggen was beginning to stir. I don't suppose he had any idea what he was wearing (I think there is hardly a man anywhere who can conceive of himself waking up in a bearskin), but he began to yell for us to get the horrid thing off of him, and in a voice that bespoke authority, hurrying subordinates, scurrying waiters, scuttling doormen, and gushing oil wells. But we were having none of his impertinence. Buck – Buck, who was rich only in brawn and friends – Buck told him to shut up. Griggen almost gagged on that.

We led him into the cabin and then removed the bearskin. Griggen looked with amazement at the thing, then peered at us in our costumes, and I guess the knock on the head made him lose his bearings for a moment, as he said:

"What have I fallen into – a time machine or a lunatic asylum?"

"Neither, Mr. Griggen," I said. "We're all fugitives from the charity ball and you're our guest. In the spirit of the evening I might say that we're masquerading as your abductors and you as our victim, but don't believe it – the ball is over and this is the real thing."

"This is an outrage!" he howled.

"Agreed," I said. "But we haven't brought

you here because we needed a fourth for bridge. I warn you, we're desperate men who will stop at nothing to achieve our aims. So please sit down and make yourself comfortable. This whole outrageous business won't take more than a day or two, depending upon what cooperation we receive from you."

"Cooperation? What are you talking about?" he demanded, cutting quite an indignant figure in his toga.

"We're going to trade you for five million dollars, and at the same time make you famous not only in the world of high finance and low dealings, but in the history books, too. You are now a key figure in the greatest scoop-up caper of all time. Welcome to the history books, Mr. Griggen. You've risen this evening from the footnotes to a chapter-heading." He was perversely unimpressed, however.

"You'll never get away with this, Mr. . . . Mr. . . . ."

"Fillmore."

"Damn you, Fillmore. You can't do this to me. It's an outrage, and besides, I can't stand notoriety."

"It's already half done, Mr. Griggen. Now, we've got beer and baloney in the icebox. Not very substantial, but homey. Won't you join us?"

Later we changed clothes, and Moses, Byron, Fillmore, and the nameless caveman vanished. As befitted a man of his economic stature, Griggen proved quite a nuisance. He was forever demanding a battery of telephones with which to call his lawyers. Only when we threatened to put him back into the bearskin and train him to ride a bicycle did he finally desist and go to sleep. Buck sat watch over him while Jack and I sat in the kitchen and drank beer and congratulated ourselves.

"Let Blue and his boys top this one," I said with pardonable pride. "Once they hear about it, they'll pull in their nets and close shop and leave the field to the professionals."

"I have to hand it to you, Bush," said Jack. "You've got genius. But do you really think we'll get five million for him?"

"No question about it," I said. "Now you could never get five million for the king of England or for a billionaire's grandson; but for somebody like J. J. Griggen, yes, absolutely – because he's still capable of making that a hundred times over; that's why whoever we contact will be only too eager to dish it out and get him back. Griggen can go right back to his desk, roll up his sleeves, and start making money again. Get it?"

"What a theory," Jack said admiringly. "Pure genius." It was a conservative estimate at best, but I blushed nevertheless.

The next morning we jostled Griggen out of bed, treated him to a free breakfast, and then got down to brass facts, as my old grandpa used to say.

"Whom do we contact for the payment?" I asked.

"I'm not saying a word," Griggen said.

"Mr. Griggen," I said, giving him my darkest and deadliest look, "we have in the basement of this cabin a medieval torture chamber, replete with racks, whips, vises, and long playing records of television commercials. If you don't prove to be an amenable client, you'll find yourself subjected to the more barbaric side of human nature. Now – answer the question."

He sighed. He was beaten and, shrewd businessman that he was, saw it. But he made the best of it.

"You contact my wife, Mrs. Hildegarde Griggen." He gave us the number. "She's the only one who can do anything. She has the key to my vault."

"Is she an hysterical woman?"

"Cold as ice."

"She'll follow my instructions?"

225

"If she knows my welfare depends on it, certainly."

"Excellent."

That afternoon I drove into town and stepped into a phone booth, about to make a thin dime turn into five million dollars. I dialed the number J. J. had given me, and waited. The phone rang and rang, and rang and rang. After five minutes I decided there wasn't going to be an answer. I returned to the cabin.

"What did you give me here, boy," I asked Griggen. "Custer's number on the Little Big Horn?"

"What do you mean?" he asked. "That's Mrs. Griggen's private phone."

"It's so private that nobody answered."

"That's not so odd. Mrs. Griggen is very active."

"Won't she be sort of alarmed at your being missing?"

"Not yet she won't. I often spend the night away from home. My interests are far-flung, Mr. Fillmore; they demand constant attention, day and night; as you'll soon learn."

I tried again, later that afternoon, then that evening again. No answer. I was beginning to get nervous about things. A man like J. J. Griggen does not remain missing for long without about a thousand people starting to miss him. Once somebody caught wise to what was going on, there would be enough heat put on to fry every egg in New Jersey.

"Didn't your wife accompany you to the ball?" I asked this creature of opulence.

"No," said Griggen. "She doesn't like those things. I wish you would get hold of her and consummate this deal. I'm getting damned sick of this place."

That night passed and then it was morning again.

"This has to be it," I said to Jack. "We either contact the old lady today or we have to let him go. By tonight he'll be so thoroughly missed that I wouldn't be surprised if both Wall Street and the Wall of China collapsed. We'll have the army, navy, Marines, Air Force, Coast Guard, and a reactivated CCC looking for us."

So I drove back to town, thinking again about the thin dime that stood between me and five million dollars. I would tell Mrs. Griggen not to be panicky, not to tell a soul, merely to go into the vault with a shovel and a barrel and she could have her husband back.

But I didn't tell her anything. Because she wasn't there. All I got for my dime was a soft, constant ringing of a telephone. Then I had to hang up and go back to the cabin.

"Mr. Griggen," I said to him, "you're a free man. Go back to your oil wells."

"Are you getting the five million?" he asked with a certain fascinated interest.

"Go home, Mr. Griggen," I said. I couldn't wait to get him out of my sight. It hurt me to look at him.

We watched him walk through the door, down the path, and out into the road.

"There goes five million dollars, tax-free," I said to my tragic-faced associates. "Lost for want of a woman's voice. All she had to do was come home from the beauty parlor or the tea at Mrs. Vanderfeller's or wherever she was, and say hello into the phone, and we had five million."

"This will become a day of mourning for me," said Jack.

Buck grunted.

Being an odd fellow, not wanting notoriety, J. J. Griggen said nothing to the police of what had happened. And I, of course, was not about to go mentioning it to people. For one thing, I didn't want our abysmal competitors, the Barney Blue boys, to hear about how I had to let five million dollars pass through the door. It would have cast a tarnish on my reputation that not even the latest detergent could have gotten out.

As it was, I ran across Barney Blue some weeks later at a downtown tavern where gentlemen of a certain stripe generally converged.

"How is my competitor?" I asked him.

Instead of the bright smile and flippant remark, all I got from him was a glum look.

"We're out of it, Bush," he said. "The field is all yours again. And believe me, after getting my feet wet in the profession and seeing what a complicated business it is, you have all my esteem and admiration."

"Well, thank you, Barney, thank you very much. You're giving up?"

"We tried something big, but it didn't work out. I guess we just didn't have your know-how. Do you know who we scooped up, Bush?"

"Tell me."

"The wife of the richest man in the world – Mrs. J. J. Griggen. It worked out perfect, except we couldn't get the old man on the phone to hold him up."

"This was about three weeks ago?" I asked, trying to maintain my composure as the blood left my body.

"Exactly. How did you know?"

"There are no secrets in this business,

Barney. None at all," I said. And for the first time I could see myself sitting on a rocking chair on the porch of the Home for Retired Vikings, discussing burglar alarms, alert policemen, eyewitnesses, and all the other pitfalls of the profession.

The Weapon

by John Lutz

"You came here to do *what?*"

"Blackmail you," the little man said calmly. He sat on the edge of the sofa, in a comfortable but prim position. Dan Ogdon had been behind the house sifting leaves from the swimming pool when the little man had let himself in through the gate. Ogdon had assumed at once that he was the mutual fund salesman who was due to call, though he didn't look like a mutual fund salesman, with his rather correct air and his contrasting polka dot bow tie.

"Blackmail?" Ogdon blinked his eyes, trying to think of some mistake he'd made in the past that wasn't common knowledge. "I don't get it," he said at last.

"Of course not." The little man smiled above the bow tie. "I get it – ten thousand dollars in cash."

"This is some kind of sales gimmick," Ogdon said. "I have nothing at all to fear about my past."

231

"Ah," the little man said enthusiastically, "but what about your future?"

"You're an insurance salesman!" Ogdon said triumphantly.

His visitor seemed amused. "In a manner of speaking, by golly, I am!"

"What kind of insurance?" Ogdon asked.

"Life," the little man answered without a moment's hesitation.

Ogdon rested his hands on his bare knees. Suddenly he felt oddly vulnerable sitting there in the cool leather easy chair in his bright Bermuda shorts. "I have more than enough insurance," he said, hoping against hope that the man would leave.

"But you don't," the man said. "I know almost everything about you, Mr. Ogdon. I've researched you very carefully indeed. You're forty years old, separated from your wife and children, and last year your income was thirty-five thousand dollars from your Ogdon Auto Agency."

"That's very thorough, Mr. . . . ?"

"Oh, I didn't give my name."

"Well, anyway, I'm pretty busy, so if you don't mind . . ." Ogdon stood and moved toward the front door.

"If I leave now, Mr. Ogdon, you'll be dead within a month."

Ogdon sat back down. "Just what company do you work for?"

"Self-employed."

"A self-employed insurance salesman?"

"Self-employed blackmailer."

Ogdon felt himself flush, then he sighed. "All right, Mr. Whatisname, just what is it you want?"

"As I said, ten thousand dollars in cash."

"Now, why should I give you ten thousand dollars, I ask you?"

"Because I'll kill you if you don't."

Ogdon was stunned for a second. "But why would you want to kill me?"

"Oh, heavens, I don't *want* to kill you, but I'll have to if you don't pay me the money. It's my business, you see."

"I don't see," Ogdon said. "Why pick on me?"

"Simply because you have money, Mr. Ogdon. At frequent intervals I choose someone like yourself and charge them a nominal fee for not killing them. If you hadn't been home today, I might have gone on to an alternate client. I'm a very busy man."

"You're insane!"

"Yes, but soon I'll have enough money to be merely eccentric."

"Get out," Ogdon said, "before I call the police."

"If you did that, Mr. Ogdon, I'd simply leave, and the police, helpless at any rate, probably wouldn't believe you. Then, when the time was right, I'd kill you. Not that I hold a grudge, but I can't make any exceptions. Not only could it be bad for business, but I'm afraid I'm something of a perfectionist."

"Suppose I throw you out myself?" Ogdon asked in an angry voice.

"Why, then I'd kill you right here," the little man said quietly.

"With what?"

The little man pulled a red fountain pen from an inside pocket of his conservative, dark sport coat and smiled at Ogdon. "With my fountain pen."

"Your fountain pen!"

"Well," the little man chuckled, "not really a fountain pen." There was a sharp, low report, like a man spitting angrily, and the lamp on the table beside Ogdon shattered.

"It's a two-shot," the little man said, casually rotating the pen-gun in his hand. "Quite untraceable and reliable. They say they'll even fire under water."

234

Fear closed in on Ogdon. Fear and disbelief that this could actually be happening on an otherwise ordinary Saturday afternoon.

"Ten thousand is a little steep," he said in a shaking voice.

"Make it $9,999 then," the little man said amiably, "like one of your cars."

Ogdon looked at the shattered lamp and tried to control his breathing. All he wanted now was for this maniac to get out of the house. He was ready to agree to any terms. "How shall I get you the money?"

"Send it in a brown envelope to B. M. Enterprises, Post Office Box 19. Make it a week from today, if that's convenient for you."

"That will be fine," Ogdon said. He was afraid to move from his chair.

The little man stood and carefully smoothed the wrinkles from his trousers. "Of course," he said, "you're thinking that you can inform the police of all this after I leave and they can arrest me when I attempt to pick up the money at the post office." He smiled cockily. "Let me tell you that you'll have a very weak case. The only fact will be that you mailed me some money – no real evidence of blackmail. You won't be able to prove my visit here." He buttoned the second button of his sport coat. "Then, after things die down, I'll kill you anyway."

"I see," Ogdon said softly, and he did see.

The little man walked to the front door and slipped his fountain pen back into his pocket. He glanced around briefly before leaving. "Nice place you've got here." Then he was gone.

Ogdon sat in a state of shock. Had the weird visit really taken place? What should he do? What *could* he do?

The first thing he did was get up and mix himself a drink. Then sat out on the patio to try to think things out.

He couldn't give that oddball the ten thousand dollars. Not only was it a lot of money, but what was to prevent him from being tapped for future payments? Ogdon tried to convince himself that he should simply forget about the whole thing, pass it off as just some kind of odd, crackpot occurrence, but then he remembered the casual, accurate shot and the shattered porcelain lamp.

Well, he had a week to think about it. He set his glass on the metal outdoor table and walked across the yard toward the three-car garage to lose himself in tinkering with his antique automobiles. That never failed to soothe him. . . .

Ogdon decided to call the police, and a detective sergeant came out to see him. Sergeant Mortimus was a short, stout man in his early sixties, with thick white hair, a red, bulbous nose and watery eyes.

"Ahh, my legs!" Mortimus said painfully as he sat down on the sofa. "Too many years on the beat."

The sergeant refused a beer in the line of duty and sat silently listening to Ogdon's story.

"That's unbelievable," he said when Ogdon had finished.

"I was afraid you'd say that."

"Oh, I believe it," the sergeant said. "You're lucky they sent me. I've seen many a strange thing during my time on the force, but those days are dead and gone." He shook his head sadly. "I retire in six months, Mr. Ogdon. My legs."

"That's nice," Ogdon said.

"Nice? No, I enjoy my work, Mr. Ogdon."

"Well, then *that's* nice. But what do you intend to do about this blackmail problem?"

"Do? Why, we'll pick up this character at the post office when he shows up for the money."

Ogdon sighed inwardly. "That's what he said you'd do."

"You mean that's what he was afraid we'd do. Don't you worry, Mr. Ogdon, nobody goes around extorting money from honest citizens in this city and gets by with it."

"Look what he did to my lamp," Ogdon said. "Don't take him too lightly; he's a crack shot."

"Crackshot crackpot," Sergeant Mortimus said. "They won't give him a gun at the state funnyfarm!"

"Should I mail the money like he said to?" Ogdon asked.

"We'll mark the bills and you mail them, then we'll close in on him and pick him up. Ahh!" Sergeant Mortimus stood and limped toward the door. "Don't you fret, Mr. Ogdon, he's in the web."

Saturday afternoon Ogdon was called down to the police station. Sergeant Mortimus met him there, a Lieutenant Sifford introduced himself, and they led Ogdon over to a small window set high in a heavy wooden door.

"Is this the man?" the lieutenant asked.

Ogdon peered through the pane of one-way glass into the tiny room. The little man was sitting with his legs crossed in the room's only chair, an air of complete nonchalance about him. His hand went to the base of his

238

throat casually to straighten his polka dot bow tie as Ogdon watched.

"It's him," Ogdon said, turning away from the window.

Sergeant Mortimus beamed.

"Are you absolutely positive?" the lieutenant asked.

"Absolutely."

"We'll have to let him go."

Ogdon stood for a moment in shocked silence. "You'll *what?*"

"Have to release him," the lieutenant said. "We have no real evidence on him. All we really can prove is that you mailed him some money."

"That's because we marked the bills," Sergeant Mortimus said proudly. "I apprehended him with them myself."

Ogdon felt his blood pressure spiral upward. "But if you knew you couldn't hold him, why did you bother to arrest him?"

"Had to check your story out, Mr. Ogdon," the lieutenant said, expertly igniting a book match with one hand, to light a cigarette. "You have to admit it was pretty wild. For all we knew, you might have been some kind of dangerous nut."

"But we believe you now," the sergeant said, "even though we can't prove anything."

"He's in our files now," the lieutenant said smugly.

Ogdon was striking crimson. "But what about me?" he almost screamed in anger. "What in the hell fire am I going to wind up in? He said he'd kill me!"

"He's obviously unbalanced," the lieutenant said. "Probably he didn't really mean it. I'd say it was just a scare tactic."

"I'd say it worked!" Ogdon said, "I want some protection!"

"If it will make you feel better," the lieutenant said, "we'll send a man out tomorrow."

"But what about tonight? You said you were going to release him."

The lieutenant looked thoughtful. "I'm sure Tweeker wouldn't try anything so soon, but we'll detail a patrol car to watch your home nights until our man gets there in the mornings."

"Tweeker?"

"That's his name," the lieutenant said. "Tom Tweeker."

"That his *real* name?"

The lieutenant shrugged. "He says it is."

Ogdon clenched his fists. "*Nobody* has a name like Tom Tweeker!"

"Tweeker does," the sergeant said.

The lieutenant walked to a desk and

240

poured a cup of coffee from a battered electric percolator. "There was no identification on him; we're checking on that name."

Ogdon breathed out through his nose very loudly and turned to leave.

"Don't you fret," Sergeant Mortimus said. "There'll be a squad car at your home every night and a man to stay with you during the day."

"Thanks," Ogdon said dryly as he reached for the doorknob.

"Oh, Mr. Ogdon." The lieutenant stopped him. "The ten thousand dollars has been returned to your bank."

"Very efficient," he said over his shoulder. He was sure he heard Sergeant Mortimus say thank you.

Ogdon wasn't really surprised when he opened his door the next morning to see Sergeant Mortimus. The sergeant was in uniform, summer blue with three huge stripes on each shirtsleeve.

"I'm detailed to stay with you, Mr. Ogdon," he said as he entered.

"It figures," Ogdon said.

The sergeant walked to the most comfortable looking chair in the living room and sat down. "Ahh!" He began to massage his legs through the dark blue material of his uniform pants. "If you want to go to work or

241

something, go ahead," he said. "Just go on about your business like I wasn't around, only I will be."

"I'm going to take a few weeks off work," Ogdon said. "My nerves are bothering me."

"Whatever you say, Mr. Ogdon." The sergeant screwed up his lips. "This isn't usually my line of work. I'm more of a leg man." He shook his head. "But my legs gave out on me."

"I know," Ogdon said. "You retire in six months."

Sergeant Mortimus gave a short laugh with his mouth closed. "Old sergeants never die, Mr. Ogdon, they're just pensioned away."

Early as it was, Ogdon felt the need for a drink.

"I guess they don't think the old sarge is good enough for the tough details any more," Sergeant Mortimus was saying sadly, "so they send me out here to protect you."

It's hard to believe, Ogdon thought. *It's hard to believe it's really happening.*

The telephone rang.

Both men listened as it rang three, four, five times.

"Go ahead," Sergeant Mortimus said. "Answer it."

Ogdon crossed the room, snatched the

receiver from its cradle, and pressed it to his ear. "Hello?"

"Mr. Dan Ogdon?"

"Yes."

"Your blackmailer here, Mr. Ogdon. It was an unfortunate thing you did, calling the police. They kept me four hours. I told you I was a busy man."

"Should I apologize?"

"You should, but I don't expect it. You think you're quite safe, Mr. Ogdon, with your squad car and your personal guard, but you aren't safe at all. I have a weapon to use on you, a most unusual weapon."

Ogdon felt his mouth go dry, remembering the fountain pen gun. "You seem to specialize in unusual weapons."

"Only when I must, Mr. Ogdon. Well, I have to hang up now. I wouldn't want them to be able to trace this call and prove it was really me you talked to. Good morning, sir."

"Wait!"

But the receiver was appropriately dead.

"Who was it?" the sergeant asked.

"Tweeker. He says he has some unusual weapon he's going to kill me with."

"Talk," Sergeant Mortimus said, "just talk."

"What are we going to do?"

243

The sergeant ran a hand through his thick white hair. "Do you play gin rummy?"

Ogdon cursed and began to pace. He paced for over an hour, his mind alive with wild speculations about plastic bombs and deadly laser beams. Finally he moaned in frustration. "Yes," he said, "I play gin rummy."

The sergeant looked up from the newspaper he'd been reading. "Penny a point?"

Ogdon nodded. "In the kitchen," he said. "There's only one window in there."

Sergeant Mortimus struggled to his feet. "Ahh! That's good thinking, Mr. Ogdon. You should have been a cop."

So it went for more than a week: day after endless day of gin rummy that proved profitable only for Sergeant Mortimus. His mind was on the game completely.

When the card game became intolerable, Ogdon would go out to the garage to work on his antique cars while the sergeant sat in a redwood lounge chair and watched with interest. Occasionally, he'd make some kind of remark: "I rode in many a one of those Model T's, but I don't remember any that shade of black.... My old dad used to have a Hupmobile like that, only his was in lots better shape."

244

Ogdon was working on the suspension of the Hupmobile now, waiting for another of Sergeant Mortimus's illuminating comments, when he heard the sergeant groan and get up off the lounge chair. Ogdon turned his head slightly and from where he lay on the dolly beneath the car, he could see the sergeant's much talked about blue-trousered legs approaching.

"Too hot out there in the sun," the sergeant said.

Ogdon pushed himself farther under the car and resumed working on a tight nut.

After a few minutes of silence Ogdon glanced toward the front of the car again and saw that the sergeant was still there. "Why don't you move the chair into the shade?" he suggested. It always annoyed him to have someone watch him while he worked.

The sergeant didn't answer, and Ogdon suddenly noticed that the heavy iron head of a long-handled sledgehammer was resting alongside one of the sergeant's highly polished black shoes. The other end of the wooden handle must be in the sergeant's hands. Only a single metal jack was holding the car above the cement garage floor, and the sledgehammer head was dangerously close to it.

"Watch out for that jack," Ogdon said,

starting to push with his heels so he could roll out from beneath the car.

The low dolly stopped. There was something jammed under one of the wheels.

"This isn't my idea," the sergeant said. Ogdon saw the polished black shoes widen their stance, as if their owner was readying to strike a blow with the hammer.

Ogdon was suddenly frozen with claustrophobic terror. The wheels were off the front of the car. There was nothing to keep more than a ton of metal just inches above his face from falling to meet the cement floor. "Is this some kind of a joke?" His words wavered with fear.

The sergeant's voice was sympathetic. "I don't want to do this to you, Mr. Ogdon, really I don't. But I retire in six months because of my legs, and I think I have a right to enjoy that retirement. So you have to have an accident."

"I don't understand!" Ogdon almost sobbed. "What's that got to do with it?"

"He's making me do this," the sergeant said. "Tweeker is."

Now Ogdon did understand completely. He thrashed with his heels and tried desperately to roll the dolly, but it would not move either forward or backward.

"You know I don't want to do it, Mr.

Ogdon, but he'll kill me if I don't. He'll kill me."

Ogdon saw the heavy hammerhead describe its deadly arc. He tried to scream.

"It's nothing personal," the sergeant said.

Metal struck metal.

Dead Drunk

by Arthur Porges

It takes a lot to stump an experienced pathologist, and even more to surprise him. Nor will any findings, no matter how grotesque, shock a man familiar with every possible use and abuse of the body.

But some weeks ago I was in at the finish of a case that made me dig deeper than is necessary in most of them, and had me tangled up in my own emotions like a kitten with a ball of yarn.

It was one of Lieutenant Ader's headaches. He and I have worked together, informally, for a number of years. Although I'm not officially connected with the Norfolk City Police, Pasteur Hospital is the only one around with a full time pathologist on the staff. That's me – Dr. Joel Hoffman, middle-aged, unmarried – possibly, because of my dedication to my work. And since the nearest adequate crime lab is a hundred and fifty miles away, Ader calls on me occasionally to carry out autopsies and other tests which the local coroner – a political hack – is unable to handle properly.

The case really began fifteen months ago, and oddly enough I was there, although without any idea of the ramifications to come later. At that time, the lieutenant was driving us back from a stabbing at the south end of town: a simple matter, with no subtleties, consisting of a steak knife driven into a lung. But on the way home, we heard a radio call about a traffic accident not too far off, and Ader decided to have a look. It never does any harm to barge in on your subordinates by surprise now and then; keeps them on their toes, Ader feels.

It turned out to be a typical and infuriating example of the genus legal murder. We found a huge, garish convertible, a shaky driver, and a dazed woman crouching over the body of her child, a boy about eight.

As we pulled up, the man responsible for the tragedy was protesting to all and sundry, but especially to the pair of stonyfaced officers from the prowl car.

"I'm not drunk," he insisted, his voice only slightly thick. "It's my diabetes; I need insulin. Sure, I had a couple, but I'm quite sober."

The man reeked of alcohol, but his actions were not those of a drunk. This is a familiar phenomenon. The shock of the accident has blasted the maggots from his nervous system, so that to the casual observer, he seemed in full command of himself.

I was busy with the child. There wasn't a hope. He died before the ambulance got there five minutes later. The mother, smartly dressed and attractive, knelt there pale and rigid, as if in a trance. It was that dangerous state before the blessed release of tears.

I never did learn the details of the accident. Apparently, mother and son, the latter leading a puppy, were waiting at the crosswalk, when the animal got away. Before the woman could stop him, the child had scampered into the street. He should have been safe in the crosswalk in any circumstances; the law is strict about that; but the car was moving too fast, and its driver was drunk. An old story.

Ader watched the interns put the pathetic little body into the ambulance. The heavy muscles of his jaw corded.

"I know this murderer and his convertible," Ader told me in a gritty voice. "He was sure to kill somebody sooner or later. A worthless guy if ever there was one. I wish we could nail him this time."

I took a good look at the man. Plump, expensively dressed, well tanned, sun-lamp style, not the kind you get out in the air. He had a jowly face with bags under the eyes. His earlier paleness was gone, but he seemed nervous, and yet arrogant, too, as if he anticipated a punch in the nose, and was ready to yell police brutality.

"You can't blame a man for diabetic coma, lieutenant," he said defiantly. "You've tried it before, and the jury didn't buy any. I'm Gordon Vance Whitman, remember, not some scared, friendless punk you can frame."

"You're drunk," Ader said. "And you forgot the 'third' at the end of your distinguished name."

"Like hell I am. Diabetic coma." There was a sly glint in his small eyes.

I glanced at the lieutenant. He shrugged in disgust.

"We've had this guy up several times for drunk driving; nobody was killed before – just maimed. He has diabetes, all right; and the symptoms are rather similar, as you know. A jury isn't competent to assess the difference, not with a gaggle of highpriced lawyers working on them."

"The juries are fine," Whitman grinned, swaying a little. "All I need is a pill." With deliberate ostentation he pulled a vial from one pocket, opened it, and popped a tablet into his mouth. I spotted the label; the stuff was one of those new drugs which, for people over forty, take the place of insulin. "Just a matter of excess blood sugar," he said, making sure the scene went on record.

"You don't seem much concerned about the child you killed," I told him, feeling a strong urge to mash a handful of knuckles against his beautifully capped teeth.

"Naturally, I'm very sorry," he replied in a solemn voice. "But it wasn't my fault; the kid ran out after that fool pup all of a sudden."

"That's no excuse," Ader snapped. "If you hadn't been soused and speeding, you could have stopped in plenty of time. You hit him in a crosswalk."

"If I *was* going too fast," Whitman explained, "it happened after the coma dazed me. I blanked out for a minute, and may have stepped on the gas."

"You can at least see that he never drives again," I reminded Ader.

"Yeah," he said wearily. "That'll cheer the parents no end. You don't know the half of it, son. Let's get out of here: Briggs and Gerber can handle the details."

"Wait a minute," I said. "What about her?"

Ader jumped, as though startled. "You're right. I'm an idiot."

252

We both looked at the woman. She was still crouched there, but now she was cradling the puppy in her arms. A low, pathetic moaning came from her throat, and the little animal, tightly gripped and unhappy, joined in with a shrill whimper.

"Look," Ader said. "You and Briggs take her home in the cruiser. Get her husband, and call the family doctor."

It seemed a good idea. I managed to get her on her feet, and over to the police car. Briggs climbed in, and we were off. The low moaning became louder; suddenly she was weeping with passionate intensity. That was all to the good, though there are limits.

It's been at least ten years since I had a patient to treat. All of mine are just bodies to be studied. Nevertheless, I always carry a minimum emergency kit, and it came in handy now. I had a devil of a time, but finally managed to give her a sedative. I'll never forget the ride: the woman, her dainty dress all smeared from the gutter; her carefully made up face a mask of grief; and that pitiful puppy's whimpering, incessant and at times shrill.

Twice the woman pulled away from me and tried to jump out of the moving car. "I want to go back!" she cried. "Where did they take Derry? Let me go; let me go!"

Well, we got her home at last, and called her husband, a college professor. He picked up the family doctor on the way, and I was relieved from duty. Briggs dropped me off at the hospital, where I found hours of work already piled up. Yet busy as I was, I couldn't get the incident off my mind. Do doctors ever get used to that sort of thing, I wondered. More than ever, I felt I'd been wise in avoiding general practice. It was too easy to get involved. For days I winced every time I thought of that poor woman and her loss.

Sometime later, Ader gave me the whole sad story of Gordon Vance Whitman III. This character was a playboy of fifty plus and almost as many millions. One of the most sued people in the country. He'd never been any good, and the chief thing of interest about him was the foresight of his father, a canny old pirate of an earlier generation, when financial morals were even lower than now. He had put the boy's inheritance in the form of an unbreakable trust, of which Gordon enjoyed only the income. Such arrangements, which unfairly protect irresponsibles like Whitman against legitimate claims, are barred in most states, but not, alas, in mine. The income, of course, was enormous by ordinary standards, and cleverly designed to make tracing and attaching any portion of it as tricky as legally possible.

Whitman had married the usual series of showgirls, all of whom were collecting large slices of his assorted dividends; but other judgments, totalling millions, were unenforceable because of the machinations of the late Whitman, Senior.

In short, Ader saw little hope of convicting Whitman this time, either.

Well, I was too busy to keep track of one more social injustice – the needless death of a child – among many. I seem to recall that Whitman's license was revoked for a long time, and another large judgement added to the list. He beat the drunk charge, since blood tests are barred here. The old diabetes story was good again. As for transportation, there are chauffeurs available for a price, and after enough high-toned specialists had testified that his diabetes was under control, this model citizen may even have recovered his maiming rights.

Occasionally I saw an item about him – he was always news. Another marriage, a startlet this time. Apparently he favored petite redheads; this was the fourth to become Mrs. Whitman.

"A few more marriages," Ader remarked

sourly once, "and maybe the guy'll be too worn out to drive around killing children!"

The accident happened over a year ago, and seemed to be past history, but last month saw a new phase of the Whitman story, and it was a lulu.

Ader phoned me late on a Tuesday afternoon. The body of a man had just been found inside a locked third floor apartment. No marks of violence; no sign of any other party's having been present, even. The victim had apparently enjoyed a lone binge behind a bolted door. He had then stretched out on the divan, and instead of awakening with a size twelve head and lepidoptera in his stomach, never came to at all.

"And the dear departed," Ader told me with ghoulish satisfaction, "is none other than our old friend, Gordon Vance Whitman III."

"Good," I remarked. "But where do I fit in?"

"We have a curious policy here at headquarters. We'd like to know what this crumb died of."

"You'd better take the usual pictures, and then bring me the body," I told him. "I can't possibly leave the hospital today. In any case, it certainly sounds like a stroke or coronary."

"Very likely," Ader agreed. "But I have

an instinct in these matters, and let's be sure, okay?"

"Fair enough. Bring me the remains, and I'll do the P. M. this evening."

At that stage, of course, there was no indication of murder, what with the locked door and all. There aren't many John Dickson Carr puzzles in real life.

The police brought me the body about five, and I got all the details and photos. It was a matter of luck that Whitman had been found so promptly. One of his numerous lady friends, unable to rouse him by leaning on the buzzer, had finally called the manager, who in turn notified the police. They had broken in, seen that the man was dead, and now it was up to me. We all expected that the cause of death was something quick, massive, and natural. I would have bet on it myself. Hence my first real surprise in years.

Now, an autopsy, when properly done, is a long and involved chore. The "gross" part, actually carried out on the table, is almost identical with a series of major operations, and performed with the same care and precision as if the person were still alive and under anaesthesia. No sloppy hacking will do; the job takes from three to six hours with a conscientious pathologist. The microscopic phase, completed in the laboratory, may go on for weeks, and could include work in chemistry, bacteriology, toxicology, and any other specialty you'd care to name.

My preliminary examination seemed to confirm the existence of some sort of respiratory failure, for the face was gray and the lips bluish – a condition called cyanosis. Nevertheless, there is a standard routine for a post mortem, so I began with the skull. The brain tissue was quite normal; no sign of a bloodclot there, which ruled out one kind of stroke.

Next, working by the book, I explored the chest cavity, and found pay dirt immediately. The appearance of the lungs – the edema and signs of severe irritation – caught my eye at once. I bent over for a better look with a 3X magnifier, and as my face came close, noted an odd odor – the faint, musty smell of new-mown hay, along with the sharper, un-mistakable reek of hydrochloric acid.

It was a clue I might easily have missed. That would have meant many hours of lab work to discover the obvious. You see, nobody who served in the army would forget that scent of moldy hay. In the early months of 1942, when gas warfare seemed highly probable, every soldier, and particularly those of us in the Medical Corps, was taught to recognize the main types of poison gas.

This unique smell meant phosgene, a deadly stuff invented during World War I. A few good whiffs, and the victim, beyond a little coughing and chest congestion, might go about his business unworried, only to collapse and die later, without warning. It's tricky and variable, forming hydrochloric acid in the lungs. Real nasty, that vapor.

I told you it was a puzzler – a man dead of phosgene in a locked room. The case was no longer one of death by natural causes or accident – not with the victim's lungs full of poison gas.

Now don't misunderstand me; I'm a pathologist, not a detective. Theoretically, when I completed the rest of the autopsy, my job was done. But when something this intriguing comes along, which is seldom, and they can spare me at the hospital, I like to tag along with the lieutenant. Sometimes I've been helpful; at worst, I'm a useful sounding board.

Well, he took me to the apartment, where I got another jolt. I'd assumed, reasonably enough, that somebody had pumped phosgene into the room; there didn't seem to be any other explanation. But I was wrong. A few simple tests showed that no such wholesale release of gas had occurred. Fantastic as it seemed, the stuff must have been introduced directly into the man's lungs – and only there. That seemed to imply a tank of phosgene, along with a tube or mask. It was a sticker, all right.

But Ader skipped that point for the moment. Instead we concentrated on the source, thinking that would be easier. You don't just pick up a tank of war gas at the corner drugstore. It's not too hard to make a little of it, chemically, but not in any form that would permit its being pumped into a person's lungs.

The lieutenant checked all the nearby army camps. We weren't too surprised to find that none of them stocked the stuff. Gas warfare is nearly passé. All they had were those recognition kits which teach rookies the characteristic odors. Harmless samples. The one big chemical warfare depot was able to state positively that no phosgene – stored in big tanks – was missing.

That left the question of motive, which gave us both a grim chuckle. It was obvious that Gordon Vance Whitman III had plenty of enemies. Not as many as the late Hitler, maybe, but quite a few.

The money angle was a flop. Whitman had no heirs. In the event of his death, the huge trust became a sort of foundation like the Ford or Rockefeller setup. Which meant that none of those judgments would be any better than they were now – in short, useless to the litigants.

Well, police work is mostly tiresome routine. Somebody had murdered, and how we still didn't know, the late Mr. Whitman. Therefore it was a matter of motive. Ader and his staff had to check out a list of more than twenty prime suspects, all people with good reasons for hating the victim. I withdrew from that part of the case; they were yelling for me at the hospital anyway. Instead, I continued to ponder the phosgene problem. I kept gnawing at it during the weeks Ader's crew was struggling with the legwork.

Their efforts finally paid off. Everybody was eliminated from the list but one woman. She was definitely It. Oddly enough, the lieutenant hadn't felt strongly about including her at the start; it was almost certain, he thought, that she had no connection with the case. But the principles of sound police work sink deep into a competent officer, and her name was added to the others. You see, she was merely the maid who cleaned the hallways and did similar odd jobs. The apartments themselves were the problem of the tenants.

She called herself Mrs. Talbot, but the

first thorough check soon revealed that her right name was Eleanor Oldenburger. A college graduate, the widow of a distinguished professor, she had recently suffered a complete nervous collapse. She had taken this job a few weeks after leaving the hospital. On the off chance that her arriving at this particular building might be significant, Ader looked for a connection between Whitman and her. It didn't take long to find one. If anybody had a good reason to loathe the late playboy, Mrs. Oldenburger qualified in spades. We were brought back fifteen months to the killing of that little boy. His name was Derry, and he was the Oldenburgers' only child. Loss of the boy had undoubtedly hastened the professor's death. Their small amount of insurance went for the widow's medical expenses – nervous breakdowns come high. A damange suit initiated by the professor before his death had resulted in a judgment of three hundred thousand dollars, but there were dozens of others ahead of it, all uncollectible.

When Ader told me all this, I looked him in the eye, and said, "If she did kill him, more power to her. Why not drop the case now?"

262

He didn't lower his own stare for a moment.

"I'm a police officer. I can't do that. I'm no judge; you know that." A crooked little smile touched his lips. "I certainly want to know *how* she managed it, but if there isn't enough evidence to make a case, I won't be heartbroken." He paused. "Husband, child – all lost because of that stinker. You can't really blame her."

"What's she like?" I asked him.

"You saw her. Woman in her forties, I'd say. So far, I've seen her only at work, not in her home, in those shapeless things maids wear for dirty jobs. I've a hunch it was mostly protective coloration. I seem to remember a pair of electric blue eyes that didn't fit a common drudge at all. But I'm about to visit her at home. Why not come along?"

I jumped at the chance. Although I was no near to a solution of the phosgene puzzle, the woman began to interest me for herself. Whatever her plan, it showed a cool, keen intelligence, as well as the ruthless judgment of a Minerva.

She lived in a tiny but immaculate apartment in Orange Grove. I saw Ader blink at the sight of her. She wore well-tailored slacks of gray material, and a pale blue blouse; they emphasized a slender but rounded figure that suggested twenty-five rather than forty-five. Her hair was the sort Holmes called "positive blonde," that is, fair, but with highlights and subtle colors. She seemed quite relaxed.

With almost insolent coolness, she insisted on our having martinis. When we were settled with ours, she curled up catlike on a big sofa, and gave us a faint smile.

"Let the inquisition begin," she said lightly. On the surface she was hard, cold, and callous. As a doctor, trained to study people behind their pathetic facades, I knew that her nerves were stretched to an unbearable tension; that she was on the knife-edge of hysteria.

Ader was brusque. I think he too sensed her delicate balance and hoped to break her down.

"Why didn't you tell us your real name?"

Her smile deepened.

"Come, lieutenant. I was taking a menial job, under very distressing circumstances. Why should I parade my identity as a fallen woman?"

"You deliberately picked that building to work in. The manager testified that you phoned her repeatedly. Why did it have to be there? Wasn't it so you could get at Whitman?"

"You know, of course," she reminded him sweetly, "that I needn't answer any of these questions without a lawyer. But I've nothing to hide. I liked the location; as you see, it's near this apartment. I could walk; I'm too nervous these days to drive, and can't afford a car, anyway. And what makes you think I'd want to kill Whitman?"

"Look, Mrs. Oldenburger," Ader said. "We know about Derry. In case you've forgotten, Dr. Hoffman and I happened to be on the spot just after that swine Whitman –"

She was deathly pale now, but interrupted him in an even voice.

"You agree, then, that he was a swine."

"Of course. I sympathize with you in every way. But I can't condone murder."

"Neither can you prove it," she flashed. "I understand this apartment was bolted inside."

"The transom was partly open. Isn't it true that you use a small ladder to clean woodwork in the halls?"

"Yes. I'm only five feet six, you see."

"Were you using it that day?"

"Yes. Did I crawl through the transom and kill Whitman?"

265

Ader frowned. "No, it's too small even for you. I measured it."

She gave him a look of mock consternation. "Oh, dear. And me bragging about my slender build."

"We don't know how you did it – yet. But obviously you found out where he lived, and wangled this job as a maid. Somehow you managed to fill his lungs with poison gas – phosgene, to be exact. It's only a matter of time until we discover the method."

She raised her carefully pencilled brows, and squirmed deeper into the soft cushions. She seemed perfectly relaxed, but I could see a significantly throbbing vein by one ear.

"Phosgene? I doubt if I could spell it, in spite of my general chemistry in college. As for that job, I had a complete breakdown. Probably you know all about that, too. For weeks I was catatonic. When I recovered, any mental effort was still impossible. I had to find some simple physical work. That's all there is to it. I'm no scientific genius to make poison gas and get it into a locked room."

"What makes you think it had to be made?" Ader snapped. "Why not bought?"

She tightened visibly, aware of her mistake.

"Can you go out and buy poison gas?" she

asked brightly. "I wouldn't know. But, in any case, gentlemen, it's getting late, and if you don't mind..."

We left then; there wasn't much else to do. She was under a terrific strain, but wouldn't crack. Yet I felt sure reaction and regrets were inevitable. And I didn't like the prospect.

But intellectual curiosity is a passion with me, so I couldn't quit. And the next day I made my first real advance. I placed the name Oldenburger. Surely I had seen some of his articles in the past. What had they covered? Then it came to me; the man had been a top physiological chemist, often consulted by the big poison centers.

I got in touch with the nearest one immediately, with highly significant results. The puzzle was solved now except for one small item. Ader supplied that, but didn't know it. It was the first time I held out on him. I merely asked for a list of cleaning agents available to the maids in Whitman's building. Among them, sure enough, was carbon tetrachloride, kept on hand to remove spots from upholstery. I decided to pay Mrs. Oldenburger a visit on my own.

This time she wore a simple dress, the kind that is tasteful-expensive-simple, if you know what I mean. It confirmed my suspicion that she was far from broke, and didn't actually need a job as maid.

Seeing her again, I realized what an attractive woman she really was. Without Ader there, she seemed to be more natural. As I'd suspected, the hardness and diamond sparkle had been at least partially assumed before – a shield.

My emotions were clawing me. I meant to prove I knew the solution, but after that – well, the way wasn't clear at all.

I accepted a drink, and for some minutes we made small talk. I began to lose hope of getting through because the woman was at peace with herself. Apparently her conscience had been stilled; perhaps she had finally rationalized the murder to the point of feeling no guilt.

Relaxed and warm, she had that rare facility of withholding the best part of her considerable beauty, and then in a dazzling stroke, flashing it like a weapon. I had no defense against it, and didn't seem to want one.

The small talk had to end sometime. I took the plunge.

"I know exactly how you did it," I told her.

A slight shadow passed over her face.

"I was more afraid of you than of the

officer," she said. "My husband mentioned your work occasionally. A new test for morphine poisoning, I believe."

I may have blushed; this was, naturally, hardly what I expected as counter.

"Thank you. And I know about Professor Oldenburger. He had a very intriguing case once at the Poison Center. Maybe he discussed it with you. Whitman's addiction to liquor was the key. It's an odd fact of chemistry that if a man with plenty of alcohol in his system gets a few whiffs of carbon tetrachloride, the two compounds unite in the blood to form phosgene, one of the deadliest of the early war gases. Now I believe you soaked a rag in the spot remover, and using a mop handle or something, reached through the transom to hold the cloth over Whitman's nose and mouth. With the ladder it was a cinch. Two or three minutes would be enough time. If anybody had appeared, you could have pulled away from the transom and busied yourself with the moldings. Besides, who knows better than a maid how deserted those apartments are by day?" I looked at her pale, composed face. "Am I right? There are no witnesses here, so why not admit it?"

She sat there, a fragile figure, with that

odd air of repose, and my heart went out to her.

"Not quite," she said shakily. "I used a fishing rod. Rufus – my husband – was a great one for trout. It was the rod," she added, with a catch in her voice, "he taught Derry on." She turned her head away for a moment.

"It's hardly a case to stand up in court," I told her. "I doubt if any jury –"

"No," she said passionately. "You mustn't say that. I've been mad, distracted. It was a terrible thing. I have nightmares when I think of putting that awful rag – a sleeping man, helpless..." She straightened in the chair. "I've signed a confession. I want you to call Lieutenant Ader."

To my surprise, I found myself protesting. The words came in a wild flood. I told her without my testimony, there was no case; that I wouldn't go to court. That Ader didn't know about the spot remover. She smiled as if I were a child.

She pled guilty, but by law a trial is still possible. I got the best lawyer in the state. I was now convinced she had been temporarily insane, and that was the line we held. The jury wouldn't convict.

During the long weeks of legal

maneuvering, we grew closer together. I never dreamed I'd marry a murderess, but, as I said at the start, it's not easy to shock a pathologist.

Jurisprudence

by Leo P. Kelley

Sheriff Patrick Caldwell, leaning against one of the towering maples and smoking his cigarette, felt the vague discomfort of a man who has missed lunch and the distress of a man facing a decision he would rather not have to make.

Fifty feet below him lay the broken body of Tracy McBain, looking very much like an unwanted toy thrown carelessly down into the gaping mouth of the abandoned quarry.

Caldwell turned to study the retreating figures of his deputy, Clint Travers, and Kenny as they headed down the mountainside toward the town and the jail where Kenny would be held pending his trial. As Caldwell watched, they disappeared among the trees, and he turned back to stare again at the body of McBain as if it held the answer to a frustrating riddle which he felt compelled to solve.

Soon, he realized, the knowledge of what Kenny had done would become the common property of the small Vermont town. Heads would shake and tongues would cluck and everyone would say he had always expected something like this. Kenny would be tried, convicted, and sent to Graybriar, the state institution for the criminally insane.

Caldwell flung his cigarette away and promptly lit another. He forced himself to think of the present and to face the facts. Fact: Tracy McBain was dead. Fact: Kenny had confessed to murdering him. Fact: Kenny was Caldwell's friend.

It was this last fact that seemed most important to Caldwell now. He recalled how Kenny, at first as shy as any yearling, had learned to trust him and to turn to him for help and simple companionship, and how he had honored that trust with a patience and understanding that had brought warm smiles to the faces of many of the town's residents, although there were those who said Kenny ought to be put away "for his own good" – a kid like that could be "dangerous."

Kenny had come to Caldwell just as stray cats and people with problems had come to him for as long as he could remember. He guessed he was just that kind of man.

It should be simple, the facts being what they were, but he knew it was not simple at all. It was this disquieting knowledge that

273

kept him standing on the rim of the quarry, smoking one tasteless cigarette after another and trying to decide whether to turn his idea into action or just to go on down the mountain and let things take their inevitable course.

Once again Caldwell went over the events of the day in his mind, thinking back to how it had all started a little more than two hours ago.

He had been sitting at the desk in the corner of his dusty office, not quite asleep and not quite awake, when he heard the sound of familiar footsteps on the porch. He lifted his feet to the scarred wooden desk, nodded to Kenny as he appeared in the doorway, and spoke a greeting.

Kenny made no answer.

"Come along in, boy," Caldwell said. "It's getting hot out there."

Kenny strode with measured steps across the room until he stood beside the desk, gazing down at his friend, his eyes even blanker than usual. He was many years younger than Caldwell, not more than twenty, with hair so blond it turned white under the sun. He was almost handsome, but his vague eyes contradicted his handsomeness, giving it something of the quality of a fresh coat of paint on an abandoned dwelling.

One day in the past, Kenny's mind had just stopped developing, but his arms had continued pushing themselves beyond the edges of his shirtsleeves and his voice had cracked and then deepened.

"Sit down, Kenny," Caldwell said. "Nice day."

Kenny sat down stiffly, staring steadily at Caldwell, who was trying to ignore the pain in his fingers. Arthritis was an ignoble affliction, he had long ago decided. It robbed you of little things, a sly thief. It made you hate the spring rain and the sight of other men squeezing the triggers of their rifles without a twinge of pain or a thought to anything other than the game in their sights. It made you know you were growing old.

At last, Kenny spoke. "I've come to tell you that I shot Mr. McBain and he's dead as dust."

Caldwell swung his feet down from the desk and leaned over its cluttered surface. When he spoke, his voice was steady, betraying nothing of the sudden fear he felt. "You shot Tracy McBain?"

Kenny nodded.

"You aren't just telling stories, are you, boy?" Caldwell asked anxiously. "You are saying the truth?"

"Yes, the truth."

"And he's dead?"

"He don't move."

"Where is the – where is Mr. McBain?"

Kenny jerked a thumb over his shoulder. "Up at the quarry," he replied in a shaky voice. His hand returned to lie stolidly in his lap.

Caldwell saw the stains, unmistakably blood, on the boy's hands. But the boy had never even hunted, never had a gun in his hands! He hated hunting and guns! Caldwell let out his breath with a sound somewhere between a sigh and a groan. "Ah, Kenny," he said softly. "Why?"

Kenny shook his head slowly and said nothing.

"Where did you get the gun?"

The boy shrugged. "It was his."

"McBain's?"

"Yes, Mr. McBain's."

"It was an accident?" Desperately, hopefully.

Kenny shook his head again. "No, I meant to do it and I did it." He paused. "I guess I'm glad."

Caldwell yelled, "Clint!" He heard the sound of booted feet hurrying from the rear of the building. Clint Travers, Caldwell's deputy, came into the room, halted when he saw Kenny. Noting the dismayed expression

276

on Caldwell's face, he elected to keep his mouth shut.

"Kenny," Caldwell began, "says he shot and killed Tracy McBain." He pointed to the dried blood on Kenny's hands.

Travers let out a low whistle. "When?"

Caldwell repeated the question to Kenny a little too loudly.

"Half an hour ago," Kenny answered. "I came right down to tell you," he said to Caldwell and then lapsed into silence, examining his hands.

"I'm sorry, Patrick," Travers said quietly. "You tried your best."

Caldwell, looking up, saw something in Travers' eyes that suggested Clint was sorry, too. Yes, he mused, I tried my best. I did what little I could. I taught the boy to shingle a roof and to cook his own meals. I tried to teach him self-respect and truth and love and a lot of other things I'm not at all sure I understand myself. I tried my best and now I see that my best was not enough.

Caldwell shifted his gaze to where Kenny sat, eyes cast down, shoulders hunched over in an attitude of defeat. He knew Kenny was really, in a way, not much more than a child. Everyone thought of Kenny that way – just a child, really. You tended to forget the brawny arms and the broad shoulders and remember only the bright smile that burst into being at the sight of a brilliant butterfly or the sound of an unseen someone laughing in the soft darkness of a summer night. After his mother had run off almost fifteen years ago, there was only an aging aunt left to look after him. When she died, Kenny was left alone except for the dappled hound he loved and who followed him everywhere – over the hills in the blaze of autumn and across the snow-smothered fields in winter.

Caldwell forced himself to think of the here and now, of what Kenny had just told him: I've come to tell you that I shot Mr. McBain and he's dead as dust.

"Why did he do it, Patrick?" Travers asked. "Did he tell you why?"

Caldwell shook his head. "He only told me how," came his terse reply. "He used McBain's gun, that's all I know. He wouldn't or couldn't say why." The *how* was usually quite enough for most people, Caldwell thought with some bitterness. People always wanted to know *how*. Did the killer use a knife, a gun, a rope – poison perhaps? The *why* was seldom as important and never as exciting.

"Maybe," Travers ventured tentatively, "maybe it was self-defense."

Caldwell hoped so. His fingers felt like
278

wood and he wondered if the pain would ever stop or even lessen. He shoved the ten offenders into his pockets as if he were ashamed of them. He stood up slowly. "Will you take us up to the quarry and show us how it happened, Kenny?" he asked gently.

Without a word, Kenny got up and started for the door. Caldwell stepped around the desk and Travers followed them out into the sunlight.

It took them forty minutes to reach the rim of the quarry. Kenny stood off to the left where the trees thinned out and the land fell away to form a plateau. They all stared down at the twisted body of Tracy McBain.

"He paid me once to take him up the trail over there and show him the salt licks," Kenny remarked absently.

Caldwell barely heard him. He was remembering Tracy McBain – a fixer of parking tickets and a man overly fond of boasting that he always paid his own way. Caldwell had heard him say as much many times: "Money talks and I'm a guy who knows how to listen." Such a remark would be followed by the slow parting of McBain's lips and his disagreeable chuckle. It had always set Caldwell's teeth on edge to note that McBain's eyes at such times remained like steel.

"You wait here," Caldwell instructed Kenny. To Travers, he said, "I'm going down to have a closer look. You stay here. Keep an eye on the boy."

As Caldwell began the treacherous descent, he asked himself why he was doing this. He knew the answer. Because he had to see for himself. He had to search for a pulse and find none. He had to seek a heartbeat and find only stillness. He had to know for certain that Kenny had killed McBain. Then maybe he would let himself believe something he did not want to believe.

Slow as his progress was, it seemed all too swift to Caldwell. Within minutes, he was bending over the body. He had seen violent death in that legendary war to end all wars. It was not merely the sight of death which sickened him now, not merely the terribly twisted limbs and the awful angle of the neck. It was because all this was Kenny's doing.

Caldwell's eyes examined every inch of McBain's body. The man was definitely dead. Then, thoughtfully, he rose and looked up from the corpse at his feet to where Travers and Kenny stood gazing down at him from the top of the quarry.

The ascent was more difficult than coming down had been. Loose rock slid away with every step. It seemed that for every step he took upward, he slid back two. At last he reached the top with the help of Travers' strong hands.

"He's dead all right," Caldwell told Travers. "Where's Kenny?" he asked, looking around, breathing heavily from the effort of his climb.

Travers said, "He was here a minute ago. I wonder if—"

"There he is," Caldwell said. He had spotted Kenny a dozen yards away, almost out of sight behind a sharp outcropping of rock. He was stooping down to something hidden from Caldwell's gaze. "Come on," he said.

If Kenny heard their approach, he gave no sign. It was not until Caldwell reached him and spoke his name a second time that he looked up and seemed to be really seeing them.

"What have you got there?" Caldwell inquired. The question was unnecessary because he had already seen and recognized the bundle in the boy's hands.

"It's Bess," Kenny replied, looking down at the bloody body of the hound. "She's dead."

"Tell me what happened," Caldwell commanded tonelessly.

"She was always full of ginger, Bess was," Kenny said, with the trace of his former smile. "She didn't mean no harm but she ran on ahead of me and Mr. McBain and he got mad because Bess chased the doe he'd been about to drop from up there on the rise. He started yelling and Bess ran up and jumped on him, barking and all, and he swung his gun and sent her spinning. You should have heard her scream!"

Caldwell looked down at the limp body of the dog in Kenny's arms. "What happened then?" he prodded, unable to look away from the dead dog, afraid that if he did he might have to meet Kenny's eyes.

"I ran up here but Bess was almost dead already. There was something wrong with her back, you could tell. Mr. McBain said how he was sorry about losing his temper and he –

"He offered to pay for the damage he'd done," Kenny said, and there was a sense of wonder in his tone. "He was going to *pay!*" His breath came in short, shallow gasps now. "Bess was watching me and her eyes were only partway open. I grabbed Mr. McBain's gun from him and he backed off and started to run and then I fired it at him a couple of times and he went over the edge into the quarry. After I killed him, Bess died. I dropped the gun." Kenny drew a deep, obviously painful breath, looked up at the white clouds drifting unconcerned in the sky, and let his breath out before proceeding. "You see, Bess she was looking at me as if she was waiting to see what I would do and I –" He discovered that the words, whatever they were, wouldn't come.

Travers shifted position, pulled a clean handkerchief from his pocket, and leaned down, intending to pick up McBain's rifle from where Kenny had dropped it earlier.

Caldwell stepped forward. He spoke in a tone so low Travers almost failed to hear him. "I'll bring the gun," he said. He took the handkerchief from Travers' hand. "It would look bad, you and the boy and the gun walking into town. Take him down and let him bury Bess. I'll be along in a bit."

The better part of an hour had passed since Travers had led Kenny away, and, still leaning against the stout trunk of the maple, Sheriff Caldwell considered the facts for the final time.

Kenny was a born loser. That, it seemed, was one indisputable fact. The boy had come unweaponed to the war, betrayed by nature, his mother, his father, his aunt. Nature had betrayed him by her unfinished handiwork, his mother by her disappearance years earlier, his aunt by dying. His father, whom he had never known, had betrayed him by his absence and his silence. But Bess had never shown any sign of betrayal and Kenny, Caldwell calculated, meeting her dying eyes, had not been found wanting. He had sought to avenge her murder.

Now Caldwell knew that Kenny had failed in his endeavour. Having examined McBain's body at close range, and carefully, he knew that it held no bullets, no bullet wound. He had reconstructed the scene in his mind – Kenny seizing the unfamiliar rifle and firing wildly, McBain backing off in terror, slipping and falling to his death at the bottom of the quarry. The blood on Kenny's hands, Caldwell realized, had belonged to Bess.

Thus, Kenny would not stand trial for murder but on some lesser charge. He would learn that he had failed Bess, unless Caldwell saw to it that he stood trial for the crime he had intended – the crime uncommitted – murder. In either case, for Kenny, it was hopeless; he would wind up in Graybriar to wear for the rest of his life an invisible sign that said *criminally insane;* in either case.

Caldwell made his decision. He picked up McBain's rifle, using the handkerchief he had taken from Travers, and checked the magazine. Two bullets remained. He raised the rifle to his shoulder, took careful aim at the corpse fifty feet below him, and fired once, putting a bullet in the lifeless heart of Tracy McBain. The body lurched as the bullet struck.

Caldwell lowered the gun. The sun warmed him and he discovered with mild surprise that his fingers felt as strong as those of a man many years his junior. He hurried down the mountainside to see if Travers had remembered to give Kenny his lunch.

My Daughter, the Murderer

by Eleanor Boylan

My daughter Pam, who lives in New York City because she says that's where theater is at, is always forgetting that the sun takes its sweet time about getting to California where her mother is at. My phone is forever ringing at times like six A.M. and she's telling me, "Mom – I got the part!" or, "Mom – I didn't get the part!" or, "Mom, can you spare fifty bucks?"

But one day comes a call that's a beaut. The phone rings about nine o'clock Saturday morning when I'm trying to sleep late and I feel around for it and I hear Pam's voice: "Mom! They're saying I killed a man!"

Well, that lands me on my feet and I'm on a plane to New York at about the time I'd normally be plugging in my coffeepot and opening the papers to read juicy news about *other* people's daughters' troubles.

On the plane, in between worrying about my kid, I had time to think about how much I hate New York. I gave it the best years of my life and what did it give me? Dancing parts in a couple of forties' musicals and two husbands, both of whom I lost – the first, Pam's father, to a drunken driver in the Holland Tunnel and the second to a redhead in *Bloomer Girl*. Now I'm a fat middle-aged dame with a little apartment in Burbank, a part-time job in a dress shop, a bridge club, a nice old widower boyfriend, and life is perfect – or was. My poor Pam, my poor baby, they can't do this to her, I thought. Because she's got talent. *She'll* make it.

In the cab heading out of Kennedy Airport, I tried to make some sense of the twenty or so words I'd had with Pam on the phone. First I'd said, "Did you?" and she'd said, "Did I what?" And I'd said, "Did you kill him?" and she'd said, "Mom!"

Then I'd said, "Who was he?" and she'd said, "An actor I auditioned with this morning." I'd said, "Why suspect you?" and she'd started to say something and the operator butts in with the "time's up" bit, so I'd just yelled, "I'll come!"

I was still trying to adjust to the fact that it was five P.M. while the cabdriver was barging around downtown Manhattan looking for 12 Murphy Street in the Bowery (yes, my darling daughter lives in the Bowery – she says it's "in"). We finally found the dump and do you believe my child pays rent to live over a liquor store in a studio with one little window so high a monkey couldn't reach it in case of fire?

She was out on the sidewalk waving the third time we came around the block and she scrambled into the cab before it was half stopped and was crying and hugging me – I wish I may die before I ever feel my heart torn apart like that again. But I just hugged her back and patted that pretty, long brown hair and said, "My daughter, the murderer." That made her giggle because it's a joke we have: I've always introduced her as "my daughter, the actress," ever since she was little and started telling me she was going to be one.

On the sidewalk I tried not to gag at the sight of the crummy-looking neighborhood and I asked where the cops were if she was a murder suspect. Pam said she was on her honor not to leave the place and Sergeant Somebody was coming later to talk to both of us. That eased my mind and I followed her up the ratty stairs to the "apartment." She proudly showed me the furniture she'd bought at a flea market and pointed out how nice the rug I'd sent her looked. She told me the kitchen area was only a matter of pulling aside the curtain (God forgive the landlord for that stove) and that a mere twenty steps took you down the hall to the bathroom she shared. I asked her if she shared it with a herd of elephants and she said what I was hearing was some members of a ballet troupe who'd just moved in upstairs.

"Well, to business," I said and sat down at a rickety card table while Pam made tea. "Right from the beginning – go."

She stared down at a mug she was holding and said: "The poor old man died right here in this room."

"Old?" I was surprised. "He was old?"

"Yes, seventy, maybe eighty. Didn't I tell you?"

"You did not." Pam was squeezing lemon in my tea. "What the hell was he doing here?"

"I invited him. Mom, he was so pathetic. He knew he wasn't going to get the part and he wanted it so much. Do you remember the play – it's a revival – *Death Takes a Holiday?*"

Not only do I remember the old tearjerker, my roommate understudied the girl's part when it was revived back in the forties. I said: "Were you auditioning for Grazia?"

Pam nodded. "They said they'd let me know by tomorrow."

She'd be *perfect*. But it was creepy to think

that the old guy had died on the day he'd auditioned for a play which is about a mysterious few days when nobody in the world can die – something about Death taking the form of a man and falling in love. I dragged my mind back to the present mess and said: "So what happened?"

Pam folded her hands on the table, but they shook anyway. She said: "We walked out of the audition together – oh, God, I can't believe it was only this morning – and I said, 'I think you read Manuel beautifully.' He said they'd just told him they weren't going to cast him and he knew it was because of his drinking. I said that I was going to walk home because it was such a nice day, real Indian summer, and it was only fifteen blocks and that if he'd like to come along we could have a bite of lunch at my place."

"You soft-hearted dope," I said, knowing I'd probably have done the same thing.

"Mom, you probably would have done the same thing. He was such a sweet old guy, a real old-time actor. His name was Lawrence Canfield. We walked down Seventh Avenue and he was telling me about when he played with people like Forbes Robertson and Walter Hampden. When we got to 18th Street he said he lived a block away and asked if I'd mind waiting while he went and got his coat in case it turned chilly later. I said I'd wait in the bookstore on the corner. I could tell he probably didn't want me to see the fleabag he lived in."

He lived in a fleabag, I thought, looking around.

Pam went on, her voice getting shaky. "I waited about twenty minutes – I thought maybe he wasn't coming back – but he did and he had the coat and we walked on down here. I opened a can of soup and I had some banana bread and we sat here and talked about the theater. Then Ruth Pearlman – she's an artist, she lives across the hall – Ruth knocked on the door to say I had a phone call from the Morris Francis office. I don't have a phone and Ruth let me take calls on hers. So I went over to her studio and they told me about an audition I could go to tomorrow. I wasn't gone five minutes and when I got back" – Pam started to cry – "he was lying dead on the floor. The police said it was cyanide."

It took me a while to get her calmed down but I felt better already. The thing was so obvious I was even getting sore at the police for being dense.

"Honey," I said, "drink that tea and listen. What could be more obvious? Has-been actor takes powder after bum audition. It's the classic story –"

"But his wallet was missing," sobbed Pam.

"His wallet?" I was getting more aggravated by the minute. "His *wallet?* Who knew he had one with him?"

"I did." Pam wiped her eyes.

I was beginning to feel like my head wasn't screwed on tight. "How would you know?"

"He took it out while we were talking. He was showing me some clippings, old reviews of some good performances he'd given."

Oh, he'd given a good performance, all right. He'd given a *great* performance and landed my kid in the soup. Rave reviews for you, buster. But it still didn't make sense.

I said: "So his wallet was missing. Maybe an itchy-fingered cop took it. Who cares? An old down-and-outer like that – how much could have been in it?"

Pam said, "Five thousand dollars," and swallowed her tea.

It's a good thing I wasn't swallowing at the moment; I'd have choked. I stared at her and said: "You saw the money?"

"Not till they found the wallet."

"It's been *found?*"

"Yes. In that closet. In my coat pocket."

She began to cry again and I nearly joined her. But in spite of the craziness of it all, what

292

had happened still stuck out like a sore thumb. The poor old gink had performed the last dramatic deed of his career. On the day he knew he was washed up, a lovely girl befriended him, he slipped her all his worldly goods, and took a powder.

But where'd he get the money? He didn't take it to the audition with him; they left the theater and started to walk downtown. Bingo! – he asks Pam to wait while he goes for his coat because the great and noble idea for the end of the act has just occurred to him.

Would he have that much cash stashed away? Not that it mattered – he could have robbed a bank yesterday for all I cared – the thing was to prove he'd planted it on Pam himself before he bowed out. Couldn't the dope have realized it might look like she knocked him over for it? Why didn't he just give it to her and then go home and croak there? But no, he had to expire at her feet. Actors!

There was a knock on the door which practically said open up, this is the law. The fellow who walked in wasn't too copish, though. I liked the way he smiled at Pam and shook hands with me. He was middle-aged with sandy hair and glasses and Pam introduced him as Sergeant Whelan. I spoke right up and said look, sir, you must remember some of those old Grade B movies with Lewis Stone we could all guess the end of – this has got to be one of them. He said I know, I know, but he wished the dead man had left some positive evidence that Pam had not (a) killed him, and (b) robbed him.

We all sat down and looked at each other. By now it was almost seven o'clock and the sun had given up on the one lousy little window. The room was full of shadows, like Pam's face. She said in a tired way that she could fix us some supper but I just told her to stay put, that I wanted to ask the sergeant a few questions about what had happened from his point of view.

He said this is what had happened: at about noon a call had come into headquarters from a hysterical girl saying that a man had committed suicide in her studio. When they got there, she and a friend from across the hall were hanging onto each other and the old gent was stretched out dead as a haddock from – examination had shown – cyanide.

I said: "How does his wallet come into it?"

He and Pam looked at each other and she put a hand over her eyes. He said: "The body had just been taken away and a few of us were still here. My boss told Pam she'd better call a lawyer and she said she'd rather call her mother and she'd use the booth across the street. She opened that closet and took her coat out and I held it for her. I saw this wallet bulging in the pocket. I said she'd better carry her wallet in a safer place, especially in the Bowery, and I took it out and handed it to her. Then I saw the initials on it. L.C."

I said: "What was in it?"

He said: "Identification, some old newspaper clippings, and about five grand in hundred-dollar bills." Sergeant Whelan looked at Pam in a real kind way. "By the way, it was all his own money. We found a cancelled bankbook in his coat pocket. He closed out his savings account at the Provident Trust on 18th Street this morning."

While Pam waited for him in that bookstore, I thought, and wondered why he was taking so long.

There was another knock on the door and a straggly-haired girl put her head in to say that Pam had a phone call. Pam thanked her and looked at Whelan. He got up and said he'd go with her and that decided me. We all piled across the hall to another studio apartment worse than Pam's – hardly a stick of furniture, and with an awful statue of something or other in the middle of the floor.

Pam picked up the phone and listened for about half a minute. Then she began to cry. I grabbed the phone and said: "This is Pam's mother. She's very upset. A man killed himself in her place this morning."

A man's voice said: "My God, then he meant it. Was it Lawrence Canfield?" My heart jumped and I said yes, who was this, please?

The voice went on: "This is Jerry Pope at the 22nd Street Theater. We had auditions this morning for a play called *Death Takes a Holiday*. About an hour after everyone left, Canfield phoned to ask if Pam had gotten the part of Grazia. I said yes, we'd just decided because she was so great, and Canfield said he was on his way down to her studio with her and he'd like the pleasure of telling her himself since this was – I forget his exact words – something like 'the last happy thing he'd ever be able to do.' I knew he was depressed about not being cast and I started to tell him I was sorry but he said, and I remember this distinctly, 'Don't worry about me, Jerry, I won't be around to embarrass you after today.' I began to wonder if he'd even told Pam about the part, so I just told her myself."

I said, "Jerry, will you please repeat what

you've just said to this police officer?" and I handed the phone to Sergeant Whelan.

Pam had already beat it back across the hall and I found her sitting on her bed holding her head in her hands. I said, "Honey, you got the part, how great," and she just nodded and said she hated herself for feeling happy. Then she lay back on the pillow, exhausted. There was a little pink afghan at the foot of the bed and I pulled it up over her and nearly burst out crying when I saw it was the one I'd made for her crib.

Whelan came in and closed the door behind him. I said, "Will that take care of it – the suicide, I mean?"

He said: "I think so. Now prove to me what we all know anyway: that Pam didn't take the money from his body."

Damn it, I knew he was going to say that. I looked at Pam but she just lay there with her eyes closed. I beckoned Whelan over to the kitchen area and said: "Hasn't she had enough for one day?" He looked upset and said she sure had but –

"But there's still this one point left." He nodded.

The room was getting chilly. I put my coat around my shoulders and turned on a few lights. Then I found a bottle of wine in one of the cupboards and the sergeant got two glasses and we sat down at the card table. I said: "You got any kids?" "Four," he said. "One of them is her age."

We didn't talk for a while. I was thinking that back in Burbank it was around five o'clock and I'd have been whipping up a chocolate cream pie for my bridge club and maybe trying on the new wig my boyfriend says makes me look like Claudette Colbert. But I was thinking about something else, too. I was thinking about actors, especially old ones like Canfield, and their vanity. (Him and his clippings!) He'd wanted to tell Pam she'd gotten the part, and he wanted her to know he was giving her his money. Then he *must* have told her – he *must* have left a message. There was no way he would give his final performance without getting credit in the program.

Sergeant Whelan seemed to be on the same wavelength. He'd gotten up and was poking around on Pam's desk. I went over to the bed and sat down. "Honey," I said, "what were you and Canfield talking about just before you got called to the phone?"

She didn't answer for a minute and I thought she was asleep. Then she said slowly, thinking hard, "We were talking about the play, about *Death Takes a Holiday*. He asked me what my favorite scene was and I said the last one, where Death tells Grazia who he really is and that he must give her up. Mr. Canfield asked me to read it for him and I went over to the closet to get the script out of my coat pocket. Then Ruth knocked –"

She sat up with a jerk and Whelan and I both froze. We all looked at the closet and Whelan started walking toward it like he was on eggs. He opened the door and on the hook inside it hung Pam's old blue raincoat – she'd had it in college – and there in the right-hand pocket was a thin paperback. He brought the coat over to the bed and we all three stared at it. I said: "Is that the pocket the wallet was in?"

Pam nodded and Whelan said: "I guess it's why the pocket looked so wide open but I never noticed the book or thought about it."

Pam said, "Neither did I."

Whelan pulled the book out, carefully by the corner, but if it was fingerprints he was worried about he needn't have bothered because later they were able to identify Canfield's scrawly writing from a lot of stuff in his flat. On the last page he had written:

"Grazia: This is all I have in the world. My holiday from death is over but I hope you live forever."

Well, the play was a success and Pam got terrific notices. Like I said, she's got the talent (if no common sense – she gave Canfield's money to the Actors' Relief Fund). And what have I got? I've got Burbank, bridge club, and boyfriend. Life is perfect again.

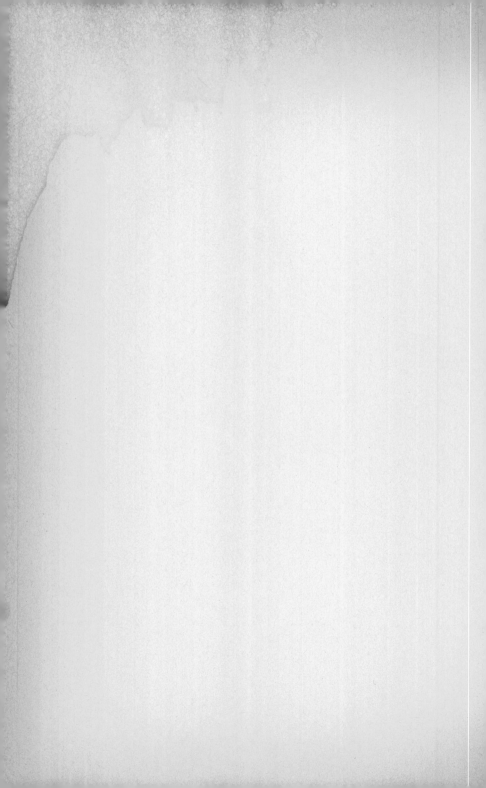